C. MATEEN

Shaylah Marston and the Rogue Roots

Cover design by Charlene Mosley

Printed in America

For permissions, please contact:

5Strongproductions@gmail.com

First edition

ISBN: 978-1-7349043-1-4

Advisor: Chanilis Mateen
Editing by Megan Joseph
Cover art by Charlene Mosley

This book was professionally typeset on Reedsy.
Find out more at reedsy.com

To my husband Larry, my daughter Saniyah, son Mhykell, and daughter, Chanilis. Thank you all for being my sparks of magic, safe space, and peace in a world that's ever-changing and chaotic. To my parents, thank you for this bomb a** DNA and for giving me a loving foundation to thrive in this world! I love you all deep DEEP.

Contents

Acknowledgement

To my descendants known and unknown, this adventure is dedicated to you too. Yes, you the intelligent, the adventurous, the misunderstood and artistic descendant. The future is yours, baby. Who you believe you are, that's exactly who you'll become. So know yourself. Educate yourself. Love yourself. And while you're at it, leave something creative in this world that will 10x the joy of our descendants for many years to come.

I love you all so very much!

Chavonne

Chapter 1

Shaylah

A dense gray fog muddled my view, obscuring the rounded sneaky storm clouds that played peek-a-boo with the dark night sky. With each blink, a wet, iridescent sheen smeared across my eyes, challenging my visibility. In the distance, I faintly heard my father's voice, his words carried on the wind. Amid the fog, I caught a glimpse of a shadowy figure, its contours blending with the night. Bellowing with irritation, my father's voice pierced the air like tiny foot soldiers with bullhorns aimed sharply at my eardrums. Relentlessly, he continued his vocal assault, but I defied his domineering commands. In good old Shaylah fashion, I rebelliously ignored him and forged ahead, moving through the path strewn with motionless bodies encased in thick, white roots toward the shadowy figure.

"Shaylah," his voice echoed again, but I remained still, captivated by the figure in the distance. Turning away was not an option.

The rain began to drizzle, slowly dousing me from head to toe. Thunder crashed in the sky, leaving behind a trail of lightning that crackled toward the ground. The roots, awakened by the water and electric energy, crept toward me, growing in size. Fear gripped me, and I took off running as fast as I could, leaving the animated roots behind.

Scared and breathless, yet driven by curiosity, I caught up to the dark shadows

I saw moving slowly in the distance. To my surprise, they were not shadows but hundreds of men and women, walking in a trance. They moved forward, unaffected by the rain pouring down on them, their faces from free expression. Peeking behind me, I saw the roots, not too far away, snatching and trapping the hypnotized people, one by one, silencing their painful screams as they spiraled into the ground. Hurriedly, I weaved through the crowd of zombie-like bodies, making my way toward what I hoped was freedom.

Finally, I reached a man who stood motionless amid the crowd. I moved skillfully until I stood in front of him, while the crowd seemed to move around us.

"Excuse me, sir," I apprehensively imposed on his space. He continued staring forward, paying no attention to my presence. I tapped his arm, but still, he showed no response. It was as if I didn't exist. Then, finally, he shifted his gaze, and his pupils zeroed in on me. He stood there, searching my face while wiping the rain away from his own.

"Shaylah, it's really you. I've been waiting for you," he said, his voice filled with a mix of familiarity and surprise.

"Who are you? How do you know my name?" I questioned, a flicker of recognition lighting up within me.

"Well, a much bigger you since the last time I saw you," he replied, his sturdy frame and chiseled features mirroring the description Grandma Caly Rose had given me. His drenched, shriveled black hair clung to his head. From the scar on his right cheek to his deep brown skin complexion, he was unmistakably my Grandpa RaKem.

"But you're dead. Wait, am I... am I dead?" I asked, feeling lost by his presence.

"We are not dead," he explained. "You and I are on the road to the astral plane, where the roots draw their powers."

"So if we aren't dead, why haven't you come to see Grandma? She lights candles next to your picture every day," I said, my mind wrestling with the conflicting realities.

"Shaylah, not a moment goes by that Caly Rose doesn't cross my mind. I miss her, too. But for us to be together again, you must listen very carefully. See those bodies back there? They are our people. The screams you hear are their painful suffering. The roots, once nurtured by our people, have been corrupted. The Parjeks *came and divided us, turning our own against each other. In this division, the sacred roots became vulnerable, and now they are being used for evil. Only a few sacred roots remain, and the Parjeks need the Charcantium stones to grow more roots for their nefarious intentions. They are holding me hostage in the cave atop Mt. Charcantium, believing I'm the only one who can activate the stones within the ancient Tetratetum. But they don't know that once you're ready, you too can harness the power of the stones and control the roots," Grandpa RaKem revealed, urgency lacing his words.*

"What is the ancient Tetratetum?" I asked, captivated by the weight of his words.

"It is the box that only you and I have the power to open. You are a Jewel and the next Darkest Light, Shaylah. Once the Tetratetum is in your hands, you will know exactly what to do. When the time is right, use the Tetratetum to find me and save Charcantium," he explained, reaching out to hold my hand.

As he did, my bracelet slid down my wrist, and the single purple gem it held glowed with a radiant light. I glanced down, mesmerized by the crystal's brilliance. It had never shimmered so brightly before, filling me with awe.

"Ah, I left this one behind in your crib on the night you were born. The other two are inside the Tetratetum. You'll need all three to harness your birthright powers," Grandpa RaKem said softly, gently grabbing my wrist and raising it toward the sky. As he did, darkness dispersed, giving way to the rising sun. He guided my hand to the ground, causing powerful tremors to ripple through the earth. The large white roots scurried into the ground, leaving behind deep grooves. Then, two slender reddish-brown roots emerged, swirling around my legs as they lifted me toward the sky.

"Shaylah!" I abruptly jolted awake to the deafening tone of Daddy barging into my room. The look of shock on his face mirrored that of someone who had seen a ghost. Following his gaze, I turned to look at my headboard, only to find my bed frame transformed into a regal wooden masterpiece, covered in thick reddish-brown roots, just like the ones in my dream.

It couldn't be.

I sat in silence on my bed, sweat trickling down my forehead, unable to believe that the roots from my dream were now tangible in my bedroom. My disbelief was short-lived as Daddy wasted no time focusing on the real reason he was in my room.

"Why do I have to call your name so many times? Did you not hear me calling you?" Daddy quipped, his large hand pressing against the door frame. Momma walked behind him. *Thank you, Grandpa RaKem,* I thought. Normally, she'd fuss at me for being late, but the sight before her kept her attention off me.

"What is going on in here?" Na'Ray squeezed past Momma and Daddy, entering the room. "Look at this room, Shay! Why are there dirt and roots all over your bed?" she interrogated, stepping further into my bedroom. "This closet is a mess. Momma are you seeing this mess? And will you stop taking my clothes?" Na'Ray ranted, snatching her jacket off the hanger.

How was I supposed to know her ugly jacket was in my closet? Momma must have mixed up our clothes again. I didn't give the drama queen the reaction she wanted, though. It was our typical back-and-forth bickering about who's right and wrong.

Lost in my thoughts about the dream I was rudely awakened from, I shifted my attention to Momma and Daddy's hushed conversation. I couldn't catch all their words, but their serious expressions made it clear they were discussing the roots. I tried to listen more carefully, but Momma caught my eye and gave me a stern look, silently warning me not to eavesdrop.

Things became even more serious when Daddy asked Na'Ray to leave the room. Momma and Daddy stood in front of the television stand, facing me as I attempted to clean up the dirt and roots from my bed. The anticipated hot seat session had arrived. I sat there, covered in dirt, clutching a bundle of leaves and roots, waiting for them to speak. They exchanged a knowing and assuring glance before Daddy finally broke the silence.

"Shaylah, your mother and I knew this day would come. The day when we would have to explain everything," he said, his voice heavy with seriousness as he pointed in the direction of the roots in my arms.

A knot swelled in my stomach, and beads of sweat formed on my forehead as he continued. "What day, Daddy? What is it?" I asked, my voice filled with anticipation and uncertainty.

"We are not like other families," he replied, and I leaned in closer.

"Great, so what are we like then? A secret society of florists?" I said with a hint of sarcasm, using a piece of root to wipe away the sweat from my forehead.

Daddy and Momma exchanged another glance before he pressed on. "At this very moment, your life, my life, your mother's life, and the lives of everyone in the family have officially changed. The appearance of those roots today is a sign that has set off a chain of events our family has been preparing for. Your mother and I have worked tirelessly since the day you were born to keep you safe."

Words escaped me as I sat in silence, attempting to process what Daddy was saying. My mind raced with questions.

"Your mother and I didn't want you to bear the weight of this responsibility. We wanted you to grow up as a normal, happy, and loved child. But because of who you are and the power you possess, which has been passed down through our family for generations, we had to keep your truth hidden," Daddy explained, his voice filled with comfort.

I stood up from my bed in disbelief, trying to process what Daddy was telling me. "You're joking, right? But why didn't you tell me all this before?"

"Shay, there's so much to explain, and we have little time before you have to finish your last few days of school. I promise after school today, we will share with you everything we know and everything we are," Daddy said, his tone becoming more assuring.

I wasn't thrilled about the wait. "So, after years of being kept in the dark, the true identity of Shaylah Marston will finally be revealed? Stay tuned after this long day of school to find out who I really am," I sarcastically called out.

"We understand, Shay. You deserve to know, and you will. But for now, we need you to focus on finishing the day strong. Ace your genealogy presentation that you've been up all night working on. And most importantly, stay out of trouble. That means you and Tray need to be on your best behavior today. No exceptions," Momma chimed in, snapping her fingers in my direction.

"Okay, Momma, dang," I replied curtly, taking my time to scrape up the remaining dirt and roots spread across my bed.

"What was that? Did you just say 'damn'?" Daddy's voice grew stern.

"No, Daddy. I said 'dang'," I clarified.

"Well, you might as well have said 'damn'. 'Dang' is just another word for it. Don't let it happen again. Are we clear?" Daddy warned.

"Sorry, Daddy. It won't happen again," I assured him.

"Oh, I know it won't happen again."

He walked over and sat next to me on the edge of my bed.

"Shaylah, you must understand this is not a game. Life as we know it is about to change drastically. All I ask is for you to get dressed for school. We shouldn't have to deal with your slow-moving pace. After that, we'll talk about your dream, the roots on your bed, and how you fit into the grand scheme of things," Daddy explained with a mixture of concern and determination.

"This is not fair, Daddy. I'm completely at a loss as to what's happening to me. Look at my bed! You and Momma expect me to just go on with my day as if these roots don't exist? Don't you think I deserve to know what's going on with me?"

"Listen, you are more than Shaylah Marston. And most importantly, you are more than what you've been putting out into this world. I know this because you are my daughter. You are great, beautiful, and truly one-of-a-kind. I expect you to be more than what your mother and I could ever dream of being. Do more, have more, because you are worthy of all the greatness that runs through your veins," Daddy emphasized, his words resonating deep within me.

"Now, it's only Wednesday. Your mother and I need you to focus like never before so you can make it through these last few days of school. We will share all we know later today. You have my word. We need you and Tray to be on your best behavior. No exceptions."

"Okay, Daddy. I'll get dressed," I replied, trying to hide my lingering disappointment. As Momma left the room, shooting me an icy glare, I sighed and smiled. "Good morning to you, too, Momma."

Determined to make the day the best ever, I knew something extraordinary awaited me. Today was the day everything would change, and I was ready to embrace it.

Chapter 2

Shaylah

After my encounter with Momma, Daddy, and Na'Ray, I sought solace in the familiar rhythm of hip-hop music. I turned on the radio, allowing its strong cultural melodies to fill the room as I rehearsed my dance routine. The mirror on my dresser served as a reflection of my movements, capturing every twist and turn with precision.

As I danced, my eyes gazed into the mirror, revealing a universe of curiosity and wonder. Within the depths of my irises, a kaleidoscope of hues shimmered, capturing the essence of the magical forces coursing through my veins. Grandma Caly Rose always said the eyes were the gateway to seeing beyond the surface, delving into the mysteries of darkness and light.

Beads of sweat adorned my forehead. I took a moment to admire my skin, kissed by the sun's gentle caress. Its luminous copper hue resembled the glow of a hidden treasure, a radiant gift bestowed upon me. Yet, it was my hair that truly set me apart from others.

My yarn braids were a manifestation of enchantment, each one meticulously crafted to perfection. Whether neatly arranged in a high bun atop my head, like I styled them today, or cascading down my back, they moved with a life of their own. Swaying and dancing to the rhythm of arcane energies that flowed within me. Grandma Caly Rose spun yarn specifically for me, my mother, and my sister, using high-quality fibers grown and processed in Mississippi. With my mother's expert hands, our hair became an extraordinary tapestry.

As I admired my reflection, the clutter on my dresser faded into a blur, its chaos irrelevant in the presence of my own transformation. The dresser itself was adorned with copper, embellished with lapis lazuli and carnelian, resonating with ancient energies. Yet, its surface was marred by brushes, combs, photographs, and lip gloss. I swiftly organized the scattered items, bringing a sense of order to the chaotic landscape.

With my room now in a state of harmony, I reached for my worn-out purple toothbrush, my trusted companion in taming my edges.

"Baby hair on fleek. Look at Shaylah Marston growing up! Thank goodness for edge control," I declared confidently, striking poses in the dresser mirror.

I gently smoothed down my baby hair with the greaseless edge control product to frame my face. It worked its magic, ensuring today would be nothing short of remarkable.

"Hurry up, Shay!" Na'Ray's voice echoed through the hallway, breaking my concentration. "Momma said she's leaving with or without you, and your bedtime will be changed."

With a determined smile, I took one last look at myself in the mirror, ready to face the day ahead.

"You look fly, Shay," I declared confidently while admiring my outfit.

I gently tucked a yarn braid back into the large bun that sat on the top of my head, still ignoring Na'Ray's command. my attention shifted to a glimmering object amid the pile of clothes strewn across the closet floor.

It was my cherished bracelet, a precious creation crafted by Grandma Caly Rose exclusively for me. The metal sparkled with newfound radiance, and the single purple gemstone emitted the same captivating glow I witnessed in my dream minutes ago with Grandpa RaKem. With a sense of wonder, I carefully retrieved the bracelet from the midst of the disarray and fastened it around my wrist, feeling its weight and significance.

Na'Ray, making her way back to my room unable to contain her disdain, made an ugly remark about the bracelet, attempting to snatch it away. I expertly dodged her attempt and made my way out of my room. Not bothered,

I delivered a sharp come back, calling out her attitude and the unfashionable jacket she sported. With a quick exchange of unkind words, Na'Ray left my room, trailing behind me. Dash, my older brother, couldn't resist adding his own teasing commentary on my outfit as he bolted into the hallway from the bathroom.

Mocking my appearance, Dash pointed at my attire and jokingly referenced eighties workout videos. Annoyed, I fired back, highlighting his own choice of clothing, a shrunken track warm-up outfit. It seemed that neither of them had anything better to do than to intrude on my business.

Taking a deep breath to steady myself, I reminded them both that it was spirit week, specifically eighties day, and that Tray and I were performing at the pep rally. They seemed oblivious to the occasion, continuing their banter down the hallway toward the stairs. Their lack of awareness only added to their already annoying personas.

I grabbed my trusty black backpack and raced down the stairs, eager to make my way to the front door. Our family dog, Panther, a spirited mix of miniature Schnauzer and Shih Tzu, stood in my way, blocking the door. Impatiently, I urged her to move aside, using a less-than-gentle nudge. "Move, Panther, dang!" I snapped, my frustration apparent.

As I reached the doorway, Na'Ray reminded me to lock the door, a detail I nearly overlooked in my haste. "I got it, Shay," Daddy's voice interrupted, halting me in my tracks. He appeared just in time, his attempt at a dance move falling short. With laughter in the air, I demonstrated the correct execution of the dance move, sharing a lighthearted moment with him.

But before I left, Daddy's tone turned serious. He continued where we left off in my bedroom, urging me to finish this last week of school strong. He insisted Tray and I stay out of trouble as unwanted attention and mischievous exploits were the last things the family needed.

Exiting the house, I hurried down the porch stairs and climbed into the car, feeling a tinge of embarrassment from Daddy's dance attempts. That embarrassment quickly turned into concern for what was to lie ahead for me and this big secret my parents were hiding from me.

As we pulled out of the driveway, heading toward Brookhaven, Dash, Na'Ray, and Momma continued to laugh at Daddy's spirited dance moves, creating an atmosphere of amusement in the car. But I couldn't help but think about the day ahead.

Chapter 3

Shaylah

I sank into the plush, cool embrace of the chocolate brown leather seats as Momma guided the car down the road heading to Saqq's house to pick him up for school. The laughter that filled the car earlier went away, leaving a lingering sense of quiet contemplation in the air. Gazing out of the window, scenes whizzed by, triggering a cascade of memories from the dream I just had and making me wonder what the big secret my parents needed to tell me could be. The suspense was keeping me on the edge of my seat.

As Momma pulled the car into Saqq's driveway, a sudden memory washed over me, transporting me back to the countless times Saqq had woven his way into Tray and I's school adventures. It seemed like he had a mysterious ability to pop up whenever we least expected it. I remember that time in sixth grade when Tray and I planned to free the frogs to be used for our class science experiment.

On that particular day, Mr. Freeman explored the captivating realms of mineralogy, cunningly singling me out due to my grandmother's involvement with crystals in her store. Although I highly respected Grandma Caly Rose's expertise in various cool areas, I found myself less enthused about discussing her shop in the midst of a classroom setting. Thankfully, Tray, ever perceptive, skillfully diverted the conversation, effectively shifting Mr. Freeman's attention away from the topic.

Today marked the final day of school, and I had no intention of spending it on discussions about my grandmother's business.

Who really cared about rocks, anyway?

Well, apparently Mr. Freeman did. He was the kind of teacher who genuinely cared about his students' interests, always striving to keep them engaged in the classroom.

As the class drew to a close, Tray and I converged at the locker graveyard, a section of lockers near the custodian's office that bore the battle scars of countless kicks and punches from unknown assailants. While most students avoided these battered lockers, we saw them as hidden treasures, brimming with untapped potential. Among the beat up row, we stumbled upon two lockers. Despite their outward appearance, they were totally spotless. With a touch of creativity and a flair for personalization, we upgraded them into dazzling showcases adorned with bedazzled mirrors, assorted lip glosses, gel pens, cell phone chargers, and an assortment of snacks.

Approaching our lockers, a sense of focused determination settled upon me, evident in the way I brushed off Tray's attempts at conversation. I swung open my locker, and my reflection greeted me from the bedazzled mirror, offering a quick pause for self-reflection. Yet, the memory of Mr. Freeman's plan to subject innocent frogs to a gruesome fate echoed in my mind, troubling me deeply. As I was departing Mr. Freeman's class, he casually informed me the unfortunate amphibians were awaiting their doom in the courtyard shed, sealed within white buckets, set to meet their fate the following morning.

"Tray, we gotta help those frogs. They shouldn't have to go through bad stuff at all. It's not fair. They are helpless. Mr. Freeman may have some weird ides, but we gotta set them from free before he does something really bad. . II said all serious, closing my locker and turning to Traylecia with a determined face.

And so, Operation Froggy Freedom was born. During lunch, we moved to a more secluded spot, far from prying eyes, carefully devising our plan to infiltrate the fortress of Brookhaven. The perfect moment for our secret operation would be after nine o'clock, when the only lingering presence within the school would be the custodian, Jonathan. With each detail ironed out, our chat concluded mere minutes before the lunch bell rang, signaling our dismissal and leaving us just enough time to remind each other to gather at the designated meeting spot at nine-fifteen that night.

The corner store, nestled a block away from Brookhaven, served as our secret meeting point. True to our unspoken agreement, at precisely nine-fifteen, Tray and I arrived on our sleek electric scooters, ready to embark on the daring mission that lay before us. Confirmatory glances were exchanged, and to our surprise, Saqq appeared on the scene.

"What brings you here, Saqq?" I exclaimed, a tinge of annoyance flickering across my face.

"I overheard your conversation with Tray during lunch, and I knew you would require my assistance, my invaluable manly prowess, to accomplish this feat," Saqq announced confidently, flexing his biceps.

While his presence irked me, we proceeded with the mission without delay. Saqq, donned in sleek all-black attire, effortlessly blending in with Tray and me, as if he had received our secret memo. Irritating as he was, I couldn't deny his unwavering commitment to our cause.

Leaving the store parking lot, Saqq showed off his skateboarding skills, only to have his grand entrance rudely interrupted when the van door swung open, colliding with his body and sending the side mirror crashing into his face. He fell to the ground, rolling around until Tray and I rushed to his aid. It became evident that he was pretending to be unaffected by the impact. The woman from the van exited the vehicle, offering her assistance, but Saqq insisted he was fine, signaling for us to mount our scooters and press on.

The entrance to the custodian's office, as expected, remained unlocked, but it was Jonathan himself who posed the true challenge. He was always on high alert, ever watchful for any attempts to outsmart him. Everyone referred to him as the custodial guard, for he seemed to possess an uncanny ability to sniff out mischief. However, luck happened to be on our side that fateful night. As we stealthily tiptoed through the door, I couldn't stop thinking about the dangers of what we were doing. A pang of regret began to settle within me, questioning our audacity. Yet, there was no turning back. The custodian's office lay ahead, our final obstacle to overcome. With bated breath, we skillfully slithered past the office, praying Jonathan would keep sleeping peacefully.

We were on the verge of success, inching closer to our goal, when Tray's foot accidentally collided with a broom, causing it to crash loudly onto the floor. Swiftly, we scurried into the adjacent kitchen, seeking a safe hiding space from being discovered. Saqq hid behind the wall, staying out of sight, thanks to the big and impressive boiler nearby. Tray and I crawled in silence behind a cabinet, our movements as stealthy as nocturnal creatures of the night. Jonathan, oblivious to our presence, scanned the kitchen, his watchful gaze narrowly missing where we were hidden. In silent communication, we signaled Saqq to make a swift exit from the kitchen, and Tray and I followed suit, careful to avoid any missteps.

Alas, fate seemed to conspire against us. As I hurriedly fled the kitchen, my bag snagged on the handle of the stove, unintentionally turning on the gas. Panic surged within me, a gnawing sense of dread creeping up my spine. With a burst of adrenaline, we ran quickly past Jonathan's office, seeking safety in the broom closet that called us from the hallway. Jonathan, oblivious to the imminent danger, lingered outside the kitchen, lighting a cigarette, unaware of the chain of events about to unfold.

A spark erupted from his lighter, triggering a gas explosion that shattered the tranquility of the hallway. The force of the blast sent the burly custodian hurtling backward, his body colliding with the wall. The sprinklers sprang to life, cascading water upon the scorched corridor as the blaring fire alarm pierced through the chaos. Tray rushed to Jonathan's side, her innate Curious Curly Scouts medic training kicking in. Meanwhile, Saqq and I grabbed fire extinguishers, desperately attempting to put out the flames that threatened to consume the school.

"Quick! Grab his legs!" Saqq commanded, his voice strained as we struggled to move Jonathan's limp, plump body to safety on the other side of the parking garage.

"Is he alive?" I asked, worried about him. Traylecia's composed demeanor transformed into that of a seasoned scout, assessing Jonathan's condition. Clear-headed and determined, Traylecia checked his breathing and pulse, ensuring he could still draw air into his lungs. Satisfied he was stable, we propped him against the side of the building, making use of his phone to dial emergency services. As we made our slow retreat to the corner store, we witnessed an ambulance racing past in the opposite direction, its sirens blaring, destined for the scene we left behind.

Our mission to free the frogs failed, and in the process, we unwittingly jeopardized lives.

The next day at school, Traylecia remained elusive until we were summoned to the office midway through the second hour of class. Seated across from our parents, Tray's backpack and my torn patch lay before us on the conference room table. We had been caught, our secret operation exposed. My parents, joined by Tray's parents, sought answers, demanding to know the purpose behind our unauthorized presence at the school. And so, we presented them with the tale of Froggy Freedom.

Mrs. Johnson, the stern voice of authority, rose from her seat, her disappointment was easy to feel. "So, you're telling me Jonathan's life was endangered, and the school was nearly reduced to ashes, in the name of rescuing already deceased frogs?" she questioned, her voice laced with incredulity.

She continued, her tone growing sterner, "I have looked past previous missteps, the lingering stench from the stinky chemistry experiment gone awry and the chaotic aftermath of the lunchroom food fight. However, this time, young ladies, you have exceeded my jurisdiction. Do you know that punishment for such a reckless and thoughtless act would be expelling the both of you indefinitely, subjecting your parents to undue hardship? The board will be in contact to determine exactly what the appropriate consequences are for you two."

With those final words, Mrs. Johnson dismissed us from the room, leaving us to grapple with the weight of our ill-fated choices. The thought of community service, repeating the seventh grade, and a complete ban from school made the path ahead seemed fraught with uncertainty. The repercussions of our actions hung over my head like a looming storm. We were in trouble, yet again. Our intentions, however noble, failed to protect us from the consequences of our actions.

With the memory of Froggy Freedom fresh in my mind, I was determined in my resolve not to let my parents down during this final week of school.

"I've got this," I whispered to myself, the words carrying a glimmer of hope and determination.

Chapter 4

Shaylah

As Momma's car idled outside Saqq's house, he bolted down the steps from his porch and popped up on my side of the car, peering into the window. I sneered at his grinning face, taking my sweet time opening the door to let him in the car. Inside, I was slightly bummed out by the torment of his never-ending presence. I so needed a break from his laughable pickup lines. Oh, how I longed to ride the bus with my friends, to surround myself in the juicy gossip that buzzed through the crowded seats.

Yet, fate thrust Saqq into my space, an unwelcome intrusion upon my peace. And so, I found myself subjected to his nonstop incessant chatter, his persistent attempts to entice me to like him. But I had made it clear— I didn't like Saqq and really didn't want to be outside of school with him either. His liking me stuck around like an unwanted shadow. Mom mentioned the upcoming pep rally, stirring his curiosity. His eyes gleamed with anticipation. "Will there be a special surprise this time, Shay?" he asked.

"Let's focus on what's really important, Saqq. Instead, tell me about your new girlfriend. What was her name again? Edgeonna?" We busted out laughing at the name I concocted.

Saqq, wounded by my joke, tried to playfully get me back, but it didn't quite land. So, Dash and I kept the shenanigans going, firing off back to back jokes, until Saqq finally said. "Wow Shaylah, that was bold. I thought we were tight. Edgeonna? Funny, Shay. Her name is Eonna, and she's just a friend, like you," he smartly answered, and in his eyes, I could see just a tiny hint of sensitivity.

The topic shifted to our plans for summer break, and I responded shortly. I didn't care to share everything with Saqq at that moment. So, I kept the conversation on helping Grandma Caly Rose at her store and with her card game nights with her friends. My summer breaks left no room for goofing around and didn't leave much time to do the things that I really wanted to do. I for sure wasn't about to plan anything that had Saqq included in it.

"Knowing my grandma, I'm sure she has a boat load of tasks waiting for me at the store," I disclosed, turning away from him to rest my head against the window, seeking peace in the passing scenery.

Saqq didn't give up, even though I brushed him off. Not letting my uninterested attitude stop him, he stayed determined and kept talking while I focused on Na'Ray in the front seat. Her attention was consumed by the art of perfecting her reflection in a compact mirror.

"Your family always seems to have something exciting going on. But no need to be so cold, Shay. You know your dad invited me to visit his custom furniture shop. I thought maybe we could go together one day," Saqq said, his expression filled with hope.

"Assume. You know they say 'never assume, or you'll make an—" I began, only to be swiftly interrupted by Momma, her voice scolding me from the rear view mirror.

"Astronaut," I interjected, pretending to be innocent as a smirk danced across my lips. I narrowly evaded the temptation to utter an inappropriate word in front of her watchful eyes. What possessed me to even consider such a slip?

With a stern glance, Momma reasserted her authority, and I knew better than to push her patience any further. "Sure, Saqq. One day," I answered with a lack of enthusiasm, and my irritation with his persistence showed in my words. I really didn't want to be around Saqq, especially not in public. Dealing with him every morning was already a lot, invading my space and messing with my peace of mind before facing the maze of Brookhaven's halls. The idea of willingly spending more time with him felt overwhelming.

"How about tomorrow? Or the day after?" Saqq pressed, his gaze fixated on my profile, an unwavering determination simmering beneath his hopeful facade.

"I don't know, Saqq. I'll let you know when I have a clearer idea."

As the car journey continued, a sudden sharp pain pierced my lower abdomen, disrupting my train of thought. Grimacing with discomfort, I shifted my body toward the cool glass of the car window, seeking solace from the mounting pain that now settled into a dull ache. I curled up more in my sweater, trying to block out Saqq and Dash's boring talk about basketball. I didn't want to join their pointless argument about who played the best.

In my honest opinion, they were both talentless, but Dash insisted he could beat Saqq with one hand tied behind his back. The thought of delivering the gut-wrenching truth—that they were both subpar—felt unnecessary.

My attention was drawn to the music playing on the radio, its melodies echoing through the car. Momma's favorite song filled the air, and she fearlessly sang along, her tone-deaf rendition causing me to press my head further into my makeshift pillow, my sweater shielding me from the onslaught of high notes. As the car bumped over a pothole, my head smacked against the window hard, jolting me out of my contemplation.

Gently opening my eyes, I was met with a quick flash of beaming white light. Taking my time, I carefully guided myself to sit upright, feeling the softness of the vivid green grass beneath me. Confusion mingled with familiarity as I surveyed my surroundings. It was the same place I had dreamed of, yet something was amiss. Grandpa RaKem was nowhere to be seen, and the air no longer carried the stench of death.

"M-Mom?" I called out tentatively, hoping for a response that would dispel my mounting unease. "Na'Ray? Dash?"

Silence enveloped me, intensifying my growing desperation. Even Saqq stayed quiet, who would usually be quick to answer. As I reached up to adjust my hair, a realization struck me—the high bun I had meticulously crafted that morning was no more. Instead, my yarn braids cascaded down my back, adorned with clear cube-shaped knockers that Grandma Caly Rose lovingly made for me long ago. My fingers traced the intricate yarn braids, some interwoven with pieces of white yarn and others adorned with pretty copper swirls, shimmering like the copper wire art in Grandma Caly Rose's store.

I paused, my gaze shifting from my hair to my hand. It was enveloped in a white evening glove that extended the length of my arm. The gloves, woven with copper swirl designs, were mesmerizing. A dark purple sparkling gem adorned the back of each glove, captivating my attention.

Moving ahead although unsure of what was going on, I took a step forward, feeling the coolness of a soft material brushing against my ankle. Looking down, I was astonished to find myself no longer clad in my eighties outfit. Instead, a long, flowing gown of deep purple silk hugged my form, its luxurious fabric a delight to the senses. As I spun in a half circle, the dress moved gracefully, fitting me perfectly.

But my attention was drawn to something else—the sparkling pond that lay just four feet in front of me. The ensemble I wore was complete with a crystal crown adorning my head, a dazzling sight that left me in awe of my own reflection. I approached the water's edge, lifting the dress slightly to reveal my feet. To my surprise, I stood barefoot, save for a beautiful ankle bracelet of purple and gold. As I dipped my toes into the water, the coolness sent ripples dancing across the pond's surface, glistening in the sunlight. I stood there, marveling at my glowing reflection, from head to toe draped in the most exquisite attire.

I looked toward a green cave in the distance, its entrance covered in thick, brownish-red roots. A sense of familiarity washed over me as I observed their intricate patterns, mirroring the ones from my dream. Eager for exploration, I gingerly stepped on the stones that rested atop the water's surface, heading toward the cave with a mix of curiosity and trepidation. However, with each step, the stones grew prickly, as though sharp needles pierced the soles of my feet. A growing awareness prompted me to acknowledge the reality of the situation.

The picturesque scenery around me started to blur, fading from its vivid brilliance as I neared the entrance of the cave. Determined to see what lay within, I pressed on, my senses heightened with each step. Just as I was about to reach the cave's entrance, a gentle squeeze on my left shoulder froze me in my tracks.

Startled, I instinctively grabbed the hand and spun around to confront the person who halted my progress. There, standing before me, was Grandpa RaKem himself—

towering at six feet and eleven inches, his skin as dark as the night sky. His eyes, dark brown and filled with the wisdom of a thousand lifetimes, held a gaze that seemed to span the entire universe. And in that moment, I caught a glimpse of deep-seated hurt within his eyes, a pain he hesitated to express.

"Shaylah, my granddaughter, you must leave this place now. It is not safe," his words echoed within my mind, his telepathic command leaving no room for doubt.

About to inquire further, I opened my mouth to speak, but Grandpa RaKem shook his head, his eyes conveying he knew my thoughts all too well. With his big hands on my shoulders, he asked me with a serious and caring tone, to pay attention to what he was saying.

"Shaylah, my beautiful, strong, intelligent, and extremely hard-headed grand- daughter. You are much more powerful than I thought. Our family is in danger with you being here again. You brought the Marston stone and cleared the darkness. But what you did last night will only hold the roots at bay for so long until the Parjeks regain control. They are very dangerous beings who seek to end our bloodline and wield the roots for evil. They do not know of your existence, believing I somehow managed to remove the darkness from the sky and sent the roots underground. If they were to discover your ability to wield the power of the Charcantium crystals, they would kill you without hesitation. It is that very power that brought you here," he said, his gaze fixed upon my eyes, laden with apprehension.

"My grandchild, you possess more power than I could have ever imagined. I know you have questions, but we have no time. You must leave now and open the Tetratetum under the care of your grandma. Inform Caly Rose that we will be together soon and that I love her deeply," Grandpa RaKem declared with unwavering confidence.

The once picturesque fields surrounding us started to blur, fading into obscurity, as Grandpa RaKem walked away. I stumbled forward, dropping to my knees. A root dislodged from the cave, gently caressing my cheek. Dizziness washed over me, akin to the sensation I had experienced upon my arrival.

As I turned onto my back, limbs splayed like a starfish, I closed my eyes. Momma's voice reached me through the haze. "Shaylah, are you okay?"

Gradually, I regained my senses, feeling the car come to a stop as Momma pulled over. Dash's concerned voice called out, "Shay, come on, get up."

With sluggish movements, I opened my eyes, met with the distraught faces of my family. Even Na'Ray wore an expression of worry. Momma, her eyes filled with concern, questioned me about my well-being, the pain in my stomach causing me to clutch it instinctively, as if my touch could magically alleviate the stabbing sensation.

"Momma?" I called out, my voice strained, as I held onto my stomach, desperately seeking relief.

"Daughter," she answered, her tone laced with a hint of sarcasm and concern.

Desiring relief, I asked, "Got anything for my head and this stomach ache?" I rubbed where my head bumped the car window. Mom thought about going to the hospital for a checkup, worried about the bump on my head. I told her I'd be okay with her homemade stuff for headaches and pains.

Momma rummaged through her purse, her brows furrowed with concern. I could sense her genuine worry as she searched for a solution to ease my pain. But before she could offer any assistance, I interrupted her, suddenly feeling a sense of discomfort and realization.

"Never mind," I said hastily, as if to dismiss the strange occurrence that just transpired.

"Are you really okay, Shay? Here, take my bracelet. It sends calming and healing energy," Momma asked, still worried.

"Thanks, Momma. I'll be fine," I assured her, though my words couldn't quite capture how much I hurt.

"Bye, Momma. See you later."

I walked toward the entrance of Brookhaven, my mind filled with thoughts about meeting Grandpa RaKem and the mysterious place I saw. Questions and doubts kept swirling in my head, but I knew I couldn't talk about them right then and there. I had to wait for the right time to tell Momma and Daddy about my experience, so I continued on toward the school.

"Shay," Momma called after me, causing me to pause and turn back. "Saqq is a really nice boy. His parents have been a part of our lives for a long time, and we value our relationship with them. Your father and I didn't raise you to be cold and callous toward people. Saqq looks out for you, and that's what good friends do. You need to be kind to him, okay?"

I nodded, a bit hesitant, and our bracelets clicked together, sending a gentle energy through my arm. "Alright, Momma," I replied, keeping my tone cool and distant. I added the bracelet she gave me on top of my own. Even though there was warmth and love between us, I kept my guard up, a way to protect myself from the annoying feelings Saqq's presence brought out in me.

With a casual backhanded high-five and a kiss on Momma's cheek, I said goodbye, deciding to keep my thoughts private. Yet, as I walked toward the school entrance, something strange happened—I started reading Na'Ray's mind. Surprised and a bit shaken, I looked back at her in the passenger seat of the car, realizing I somehow tapped into her thoughts, which felt like I crossed a line and left me feeling uneasy.

Na'Ray seemed to think I was going to get my period and wasn't ready. Meeting her with a cold gaze, I said, "No, I'm not."

Na'Ray looked surprised too, like we both just figured something out without saying it. Did I really read her mind? I looked at Momma, who was still chatting with Na'Ray. I felt confused and a little uneasy, like I found something new inside me that I didn't understand. I had stumbled upon a hidden power within myself.

Brushing off the weird moment, I rushed to the school entrance, wanting to get away from the strange things that kept happening to me. School, with its usual routines and things to do, felt like a safe place to take a break from the mysterious stuff I saw.

Chapter 5

Shaylah

"Late again, Miss Marston?" Mrs. Fortra's voice chimed, her tone laced with mild exasperation. As I hurried to my seat, a bit out of breath from running to her classroom, she tapped her watch with a little scolding look.

"I was having trouble with my locker again," I replied, desperately trying to catch my breath.

"That has been your excuse since the beginning of the school year, Miss Marston," Mrs. Fortra remarked, finally pausing to take a breath after her epic punctuality lecture. "I see you and your friend Traylecia in the hallway, chatting away as if you have all the time in the world. Remember, high school won't be as forgiving as I am. Now, fetch your lab coat. I don't want you ruining your pretty little outfit. It's experiment time."

Mrs. Fortra always granted me leniency when it came to tardiness. She gave me an inch, and I gladly took a mile. I could never fathom why she let me slide so often. Maybe it was because I got good grades or because I was always super excited about doing random, sometimes risky, and even stinky experiments.

You've got this, Shay. No explosions or stink bombs today.

Heading toward the back of the classroom, Mrs. Fortra made her way to a cart draped in white plastic. Each day, she would surprise us with a new experiment, and I eagerly awaited to see what was in store. Her pet newt, Chaco, perched on a custom crushed velvet pillow she secured to her shoulder with Velcro, observing the world with its beady eyes.

"It's an ice cream party!" Mrs. Fortra exclaimed as she dramatically unveiled the cart, revealing a mountain of dry ice with pockets of different flavored ice creams nestled in between. Beneath the cart, bags of individually wrapped toppings awaited us—chocolate bars, gumdrops, taffy, fruit chews, and cookie crumbles.

Mrs. Fortra, the leader of the Curious Curly Scouts Tray and I joined when we were young girls, exuded boundless energy and encouragement. Her class was a source of motivation and challenge, constantly pushing us beyond the realms of boredom. Learning about the periodic table of elements, molecules, and matter never felt dull under her guidance. Each lesson was accompanied by a rap, an experiment, or a movie bridging the gap between theory and practice. She was a whole mood, and her class was the perfect distraction from my recurring dream, the echoes of Na'Ray's thoughts, and the enigma of a newfound identity.

Joining the line for ice cream, I couldn't resist the allure of chocolate with a generous sprinkle of peanuts on top. As we indulged in the frozen treats, we played charades until the very last moments of class. Mrs. Fortra eventually called an end to the game, transforming the classroom for her grand end-of-year performance.

With the door closed and the lights dimmed, all eyes turned toward Mrs. Fortra as a spotlight illuminated her presence. The end-of-year show was going to be so much fun, with Mrs. Fortra trying out the coolest dances for her performance. It was a time to just enjoy, a short break before the most ordinary class—English.

"Shaylah, I'm going to miss reading your stories," Mr. Demay praised me as I entered his class. "I've been teaching for over twenty years, and I've never come across a student with such exceptional writing skills. I guarantee your high school and college instructors will echo my sentiments. Great job!"

Although Mr. Demay often commended my writing abilities, it was the last thing I wanted to focus on that day. "Today feels like one of those Shakespearean days—a classic love story," Mr. Demay declared all fancy-like. Marcus, our self-appointed student advocate, scanned the room, waiting for someone to admit they wanted this.

"We're not diving into Shakespeare, Marcus," Mr. Demay said with a touch of sarcasm, addressing the whole class. "But if y'all really itching for it, we could always throw in a Shakespearean play of some sort to end the day."

"Please, not Shakespeare. Who even asked for that?" Marcus shot back, sparking thunderous laughter from the class.

"We're going with "Lean on Me," a classic movie," Mr. Demay declared, shutting down any Shakespearean talk. Marcus's comment unintentionally set our movie choice.

"Classic, as in one of those black and white old people movies?" Marcus fired back, accompanied by more laughter.

"Believe it or not, Marcus, *Lean on Me* is highly relevant to the pressures you all face now and will continue to face in high school. Of course, we could always pivot to Shakespeare if that's what you truly desire," Mr. Demay cleverly suggested, leaving the decision in Marcus's hands.

"Shut up, Marcus. Mr. Demay, put him in another room with Shakespeare. The rest of us will watch *Lean on Me*," Shanita interjected, rolling her eyes at Marcus.

"Great choice, class. *Lean on Me* it is. We might not be able to finish the movie, but my classroom will be open during both lunch hours if any of you want to continue watching until the end."

As the dismissal bell rang, signaling the end of class, Mr. Demay extended an invitation for us to return during lunch. I knew I had no intention of going back and bid him farewell as I exited the classroom.

True to our routine, Traylecia was waiting for me at the familiar fork in the hallway. We usually walked together to our government class, but today, we had a pep rally to attend.

"Tray, are you ready? We're going to rock it!" I exclaimed, giving her a backhanded high-five. "I just hope I don't forget to step up when it's time." I rehearsed the dance moves in my head, nerves getting the best of me.

"Shay, you've got this. We're going to go viral!" Traylecia reassured me, mimicking holding a phone in her hand to record the moment.

"Viral? Girl, that makes me even more nervous. But hey, if I forget to step up, I'll just improvise like it was meant to be."

"Meant to be, just like TLC, hey!" Tray and I chimed in unison, making our way toward the gymnasium. We had always been each other's cheerleaders— I attended Tray's archery events, where she stood out as the only Black female archer, and she never missed a chance to support me in my karate competitions. We thrived on each other's energy.

Tray glanced at my face and sensed the apprehension. Mrs. Johnson, our animated principal, began her speech, and the anticipation in the gymnasium grew.

Mrs. Johnson thanked everyone for their contributions to the successful school year. The first event on the agenda was a three-on-three basketball game, pitting teachers against students. Mrs. Fortra, Mr. Demay, and Mr. Thomas faced off against Saqq, Marcus, and Nick. Dash, our competitive friend, showed no mercy as he executed a crossover dribble move on Mr. Demay, sending him crashing to the ground. The entire gymnasium erupted in laughter.

After the teachers' defeat in the basketball game, teams were assembled for a relay race. The stakes were high, with bragging rights and the loser serving breakfast and lunch to the winners on the first day of the next school year. The teachers, determined to break their six-year losing streak, lined up alongside the students.

At the bucket toss, Mr. Demay skillfully landed the bean bag in the bucket, but Saqq managed to finish first, passing the baton to Marcus. Clumsily hopping in the potato sack, Marcus stumbled his way to the next obstacle, leaving Mr. Thomas trailing behind. Geni eagerly awaited the baton from Saqq, with Mrs. Fortra close on her heels. The students erupted in excitement, demanding a non-chemistry teacher to challenge Geni. Their wish was granted, and Mrs. Johnson, the principal, stepped up to face her.

The entire gymnasium filled with cacophonous noise, making it difficult for both Geni and Mrs. Johnson to hear the questions. Time ran out, and their answers were counted aloud. To break the tie, a dart bullseye game was chosen. The teachers rallied around Mrs. Sandy, the lively and vibrant theater teacher, while I nominated Tray, showcasing her exceptional archery skills. Tray confidently took her position beside Mrs. Sandy, and with a steady aim, she hit the red bullseye balloon.

Mrs. Johnson took to the microphone, congratulating Tray for securing the victory for the students. The support staff swiftly cleared the gymnasium's center, preparing for our much-anticipated performance. The lights dimmed, and the spotlight illuminated us as we stood in formation, ready to showcase our routine. This time, I was the dance captain, entrusted with leading the dance.

"You all are in for a treat. Without further ado, get on your feet for Mr. Shawn and the Brookhaven Dance Team!" Mrs. Johnson's voice resonated through the gymnasium.

Mr. Shawn, our school's dance teacher, approached me before I took my position at the front of the line. With a slight bow of his head, he retreated to his front-row seat. The music started, and all my doubts faded away. Each move flowed effortlessly as I danced, hitting every step with precision and grace. It was almost perfect—until my foot slid, unexpectedly sending me into the splits. The gym erupted in cheers and applause, and some of my classmates even rushed onto the floor, lifting me high in the air. Mr. Shawn joined in the celebration, cheering us on and mimicking our dance moves.

Adrenaline coursed through my veins as the entire gymnasium chanted my name. "Shaylah, Shaylah, Shaylah." It was the first time I truly felt accepted and appreciated by my peers, who I thought paid no mind to my existence.

As the performance concluded, I sat on the first row of the bleachers, catching my breath. The overwhelming feeling of success washed over me.

"Shay, are you there? Earth to Shay. Hello," Traylecia said, waving her hand in front of my face to snap me out of my reverie. My gaze was fixated on the bracelet adorning my wrist—a strange purple pulsating hue emanating from it, captivating my attention.

Traylecia draped her arm around my shoulder. "Shay, you killed it out there today. I was so engrossed in watching you that I almost forgot my own steps," she exclaimed, laughing.

"Thank you, Tray. Girl, I was dancing so hard I think I pulled a muscle or something," I replied, laughing along with her.

"Ha, not a muscle pull, but maybe a cramp from all that vigorous movement," Traylecia retorted, playfully pulling me off the bleachers to engage in our signature dance moves.

"Ladies, you both did an amazing job today," Mr. Shawn applauded as he approached us. "Shaylah, I wish you had tried out for captain more often. You're a natural-born leader."

Gathering our belongings, we made our way out of the gymnasium with the rest of the students, heading toward the lunchroom. Personal space was a luxury we couldn't afford, as we jostled against one another like a herd of livestock making their way to the feeding trough. The lunchroom buzzed with noise, and teachers attempted to restore order amid the chaos. Finding a seat became a challenge as we retrieved our lunch trays from the conveyor belts.

"Hey, Shaylah," Traylecia whispered as we navigated the crowded lunchroom, searching for an available table. "Did you start your period? There's a big red stain on the back of your pants."

"Tray, stop joking around. That's not something to kid about," I responded, smirking, as I rushed to secure our spot at the empty table we affectionately called the desert table. The desert table was reserved for teachers during lunchtime. Swiftly, I tied my sweater around my waist, concealing the stain. The whispers and stares from our classmates were impossible to ignore as we stood near the dessert table.

"Ha, look who's in the desert," Geni joked as she passed by, accompanied by her mean-spirited friends, Melissa and Lanae. I had never gotten along with any of them, especially Geni.

I glared at them, mustering the meanest side-eye I could manage. The audacity for Geni to even utter a word. I hadn't told anyone about catching her discreetly eating her snot boogers after blowing her nose.

"Well, well, well. Look who's in the desert on the last day of school," Marcus chimed in, walking toward us with his lunch tray in hand.

I couldn't bear another stare or comment from anyone. Letting my dad down on the last day of school was not part of my plan. Traylecia and I experienced our fair share of isolation after our failed Froggy Freedom operation, and I just performed on stage like never before. So, I did what any girl would do.

"What are you all looking at?" I snapped, annoyance dripping from my words. "Didn't your mothers teach you any manners? Just so you know, it's impolite to stare." I snatched my backpack from the floor, nearly stumbling in the process, and grabbed my lunch tray from the table. "Ugh, I'm so glad I don't have to witness you eating boogers anymore," I pointed sharply at Geni. "And you, Marcus Fartcus, you stinky little boy, I'd suggest keeping quiet if I were you."

The cafeteria lit up with loud laughs. The sound was so deafening Mrs. Fortra had to intervene, her voice echoing through the loudspeakers. "Settle down and use your indoor voices. You two ladies, move along to your seats." She escorted Traylecia and me away from the desert table.

"Shay, that was epic!" Traylecia exclaimed, giving me a backhanded high-five as we made our way to our designated lunch table. Laughter accompanied us all the way. Then, a sudden realization struck me. I remembered why we initially stopped at the desert table. Without wasting a moment, I grabbed my backpack and bolted through the cafeteria, leaving Traylecia behind and nearly colliding with Mrs. Fortra against the wall.

"Shaylah Marston!" Mrs. Fortra's voice cut through the air, instantly halting me in my tracks. I screeched to a stop, almost leaving skid marks on the freshly polished hallway floors. "Stop running in the hallway," she admonished, her tone a mix of understanding and annoyance.

"Sorry, Mrs. Fortra, my apologies. But I really have to go," I pleaded, urgency evident in my voice.

She looked at me with a mixture of understanding and warning, saying, "Don't let it happen again, or there will be consequences."

Ignoring her words, I rushed toward the bathroom, my heart pounding in my chest. I had to see if it was true.

Chapter 6

Shaylah

In the cramped bathroom stall, I sat on the toilet seat I strategically lined with tissue. I looked down at my underwear, my heart relieved that it wasn't the red crimson sign of womanhood Momma warned me of. Instead, whatever I sat on stayed on the back of my pants.

"Whew. False alarm." I laughed, my voice echoing in the confined space.

The bathroom remained empty, as the rest of the students stayed in the lively cafeteria for lunch.

I placed my backpack on my lap, noticing it was kinda heavy for its size. I dug inside, feeling my hands move past notebooks and a planner until I grabbed the brown satchel drawstring bag. It resembled the ones Grandma Caly Rose sold at her store, but this one was extra special. Its silk fabric bore a geometric emblem embossed in copper, with emerald-green drawstrings tied in a perfect bow.

Momma gave me this bag on the day we had "the talk," the conversation about becoming a young woman and starting my period. She planned everything meticulously, instructing me to open the bag when the time was right.

"Shay, I'm going to put this drawstring bag in your backpack. When it's time, open the bag. It will guide you because I know you might get nervous and forget

everything we just talked about," Momma said.

I couldn't help but wonder what could be inside the bag. With a mix of curiosity and a bit of excitement, I untied the drawstrings and peeked inside, my eyes getting big with amazement.

The bag's contents were color-coded and had clear labels, showing me exactly what to do. The first item that caught my attention was a copper-colored envelope addressed to me, its seal bearing the same geometric emblem.

I carefully opened the envelope and started reading what was inside.

Dear Shay,

Today is the day you become a young lady. In this bag, you will find cleansing wipes to freshen up, clean underwear, pants, and, of course, pads. After cleaning yourself up and getting dressed, flush the toilet twice. Use the color-coded bag to wrap your soiled underwear and pants. Put the empty packaging in its wrapper, and most importantly, put everything back into the drawstring bag. Do not leave anything behind. Return the bag to the secret compartment, and we will take care of everything later. Do not go to the office to call me. Go straight to class, and remember, do not tell anyone, not even Tray. Carry on with your day as if nothing happened, and I'll be there to pick you up after school as usual.

Love, Momma

I carefully placed all of the contents back inside the pouch, thankful I didn't have to use any of them.

After flushing the toilet and washing my hands, I heard the rush of water cascading down the toilet bowl, drowning out the trickle of the water from the sink. Just as I turned to leave the bathroom, Geni Port emerged from one of the stalls, her presence an unwelcome intrusion.

"Still being a weirdo?" Geni teased, her voice dripping with condescension.

We stared each other down in the bathroom mirror, trading unfriendly glances. I had no desire to fight with her at that moment. All I wanted was to ensure she didn't hear or see anything.

"Like I thought, still being a weirdo," she mocked, a malicious giggle escaping her lips as she washed her hands.

"You're lucky I have a future to look forward to and don't want to be late for class," I shot back, determination fueling my words as I walked out of the bathroom.

"Shay, are you okay? You didn't even come back to finish your lunch or see Geni rushing to the bathroom with grapes smashed all over her," Traylecia panted, having scurried through the hallway to catch up with me.

"Oh, shoot," I exclaimed, suddenly remembering something I left behind.

Hastily, I retraced my steps, heading back to the bathroom. As I entered, I spotted Geni holding my drawstring bag, attempting to open it. Reacting instinctively, I lunged forward, my arm outstretched, fueled by an unexpected surge of energy coursing through my veins. With a swift motion, I yanked the bag from her grasp.

"You didn't have to snatch it," Geni shot back, her voice showing she was pretty annoyed.

"And you shouldn't touch things that don't belong to you," I responded coldly, then quickly left the bathroom.

"You would never believe it, but it was a false alarm. I sat on something red on the bench at the pep rally. For a minute, I thought you placed it there for me," I explained to Traylecia as we walked through the hallway, resuming our journey to our favorite class, the one we shared: music with Mr. Craig.

His infectious passion for all things music made it a joy to be in his class. As we entered, the vibrant atmosphere enveloped us, and I offered a wave to everyone, including Mr. Craig, my favorite teacher.

After his class was over, Tray and I quickly gathered our things to leave. Walking out his door, confusion etched its way onto our faces as we heard Mrs. Sharnett, the office assistant, calling my name over the loudspeaker.

"Shaylah Marston, please report to the office with your belongings!"

Traylecia and I exchanged puzzled glances, shrugging our shoulders in unison.

"See you tomorrow, Ms. Marston!" Mr. Craig energetically called out.

Making my way toward the office, I opened the hallway doors to the staircase to see my arch nemesis, Geni.

"Ugh," Geni scoffed, her voice oozing with dislike as she climbed the stairs.

"You have a lot of nerve," I fired back, my tone laced with sarcasm as I took a few steps closer to her.

"I'd rather be a weirdo than eat stuff that grows in doo-doo," I taunted, pinching my nose and strolling down the staircase.

Standing shoulder to shoulder, we stood on the brink of a showdown. Our backpacks brushed against each other, creating a momentary connection. I felt a burst of power coming from the bracelet on my wrist, a mysterious flow through my veins. And then, in an instant, Geni lost her footing, losing her balance. Instinctively, I reached out and grabbed her arm, preventing her from tumbling backward down the stairs.

"You still suck," Geni spat ungratefully, finally regaining her footing.

"A simple thank you for saving my life would do," I replied, my voice tinged with disappointment. "You're pathetic, Geni."

As I continued on my way to the office, leaving Geni in stunned disbelief, I couldn't help but wonder about the strange powers that seemed to have awakened within me. It was as if the bracelet and the surge of energy were linked, this amazing thing that I didn't really get.

Entering the office, I was met with the radiant presence of Momma, her beauty shining brighter than ever. Her braids interwoven with strands of copper yarn glistened under the office lights, an exquisite sight to behold. The flawless caramel hue of her skin reflected the sunlight peeking through the blinds, while her round face held an air of serenity. The moles around her green eyes resembled constellations, mapping out a universe of love and protection.

"Hey, Shay," Momma greeted me with a mixture of love and concern. "I know you were looking forward to finishing the day, but I'm here to take you home early. We need to swing by Kaman Plaza." Momma continued, "Mrs. Shaad mentioned how amazing you were in your performance today. I couldn't be prouder."

Feeling the warmth of Momma's words, I said my goodbyes to the office staff, who looked at Momma with admiration for her radiant presence. As we ventured toward the car, a sense of anticipation washed over me. I had something important to share with Momma and I know she and Daddy needed to share something with me too.

"You just don't know how happy I am to see you, Momma. There's something I need to tell you," I whispered, our words enveloped by the quietness.

"Shaylah, before you start, I just want you to know the talk your dad mentioned he would have with you after school is actually happening as soon as we get to Kaman Plaza. It can't wait. Plus, your Grandma Caly Rose is eager to see you," Momma affirmed while nervousness touched her face as we got into the car. A strong feeling of uneasiness came from Momma. Her face showed she was carrying a lot of worry, her eyes had both a mixture of anticipation and nervousness. I, too, felt my heart flutter with nerves, uncertain of what lay ahead. Momma spoke, and you could hear a bit of worry in her voice. She told me about a girl who went out her way to bump into her just outside the office, and it got me curious. It didn't take long for me to figure out it was Geni, only someone as mean as her could make Momma react like that. As we drove, I felt a mix of frustration and excitement. I really wanted to leave Geni and her negativity behind. Her mean ways caused enough problems all school year. The tension between us was like electricity, and when we met on the stairs again, it felt like a big clash.

My mind raced with questions, trying to piece together the puzzle of events that unfolded. *What had Geni been up to now? What schemes or spiteful acts lay in her wake?* The mere thought of her made my blood boil and sent a shiver down my spine, a reminder of the animosity she harbored toward me.

In that moment, Geni and her malicious ways didn't matter. I knew deep down I could rely on the unwavering love and support of my extraordinary Momma to get me through the rest of the day.

Chapter 7

Geni

I watched Shaylah leave the lunchroom in a hurry, my dislike for her getting stronger every moment. She acted like she was better than everyone else, like she thought she was the ultimate gift from the universe. While I sat, eating my lunch, I suddenly felt a wet, slimy substance strike my back. "Who threw that?" I yelled, my voice echoing throughout the room. I was ready to face whoever was responsible.

Silence hung around in the air and the other kids stared at me like I had three extra heads. Fed up, I stomped out of the lunchroom, wanting to clean my dirty shirt. As I walked down the hallway to the restroom, I felt something slippery sliding down the middle of my forehead. It turned out to be a crushed grape, a clear sign of the attack. I was so mad that I couldn't take it anymore. I hit the locker with my fist, feeling the pain shoot through my knuckles as they swelled up.

Quietly, I entered a bathroom stall, aware that I wasn't alone. Slowly, I removed my sweatshirt, adorned with grape stains. Using a tissue, I carefully cleaned the lingering chunks of fruit from my attire. Then, in the quiet space, I heard hushed whispers and nearly silent sniffles coming from the stall next to me. All I could see were some brightly colored leg warmers, confirming what I suspected. There was only one person who could be doing this self-talk—Shaylah Marston. Who was she whispering to? Knowing that Shaylah was whispering to herself and crying, sounding upset in the bathroom stall, made me feel satisfied and lifted my spirits. Lost in my moment of triumph, I heard the toilet flush, and I saw Shaylah fixing herself before going to the sink. I walked out of the bathroom stall, feeling a newfound confidence.

As I approached the sink, our eyes met in the mirror's reflection, brimming with animosity. Insulting words were exchanged between us before Shaylah stormed out of the bathroom. In the midst of all that chaos, something shiny on the floor caught my eye, right where Shaylah was washing her hands. Curiosity got the best of me, so I moved closer. *Could it be what I think it is? It couldn't possibly be.*

Right there on the bathroom floor lay a little silk bag, with a copper emblem on the front, just like the ones my mother always told me to be on the lookout for. I bent down and picked it up, trying to untie the drawstrings. But, sadly, the bag wouldn't open. What kind of magic was this?

"I believe that belongs to me," Shaylah mocked, grabbing the pouch from my hand with a mean look before storming out of the bathroom. I hadn't even noticed her coming in; I was so focused on what I found.

As I washed my hands, confusion swept over me. Why would Shaylah have something like that? She couldn't possibly be a Jewel. She was far too strange for that.

Walking down the hallway toward the office, I caught sight of Shaylah and her weirdo best friend engaged in conversation. *Why wouldn't that pouch open?*

I stood there impatiently, waiting for Mrs. Shaad, the office secretary, to conclude her non-school-related telephone call. "Mrs. Shaad, I need to call my mom. It's an emergency."

"What's the emergency this time, Geni?" Mrs. Shaad inquired wearily.

"I need to call my mom. It's lady issues, you know," I replied, urgency lacing my voice.

"Very well, make it quick. But remember, the last time you used the school phone, you called your friend," Mrs. Shaad recalled.

Dialing my mother's number, disbelief was etched upon my face. Shaylah couldn't be the one.

"Momma, you won't believe what just happened to me. This girl at school had a pouch with one of those signs on it."

"What sign are you referring to, Geni?" my mother inquired, as though she had forgotten what she had trained me to watch out for.

"Momma, you know the sign, the one from the stories you told me about... you know where."

"What?" Suddenly, her attention was fully captivated. "Who had it?"

"The girl I despise. And listen to this, Momma, I tried to open it forcefully, but it wouldn't budge. I know this is it."

"Alright, Geni. I'm picking you up from school today. I need you to show me the girl."

Ending the call, I turned to leave the office. A graceful woman entered.

"Mrs. Marston!" Mrs. Shaad greeted her warmly as she approached the desk. Going out of my way, I intentionally bumped into her. Yes, it was Shaylah's mother.

"You're excused," I replied rudely, rolling my eyes as I walked away, enjoying the sassy moment.

Shaylah's mother was very pretty but her daughter didn't look anything like her. It was the first time I had seen her. If only she knew how much I disliked her daughter.

Making my way back to class, I pushed through the door leading to the stairway. At the top of the stairs Shaylah was coming toward me. I wanted to push her down the stairs, to witness her legs give way beneath her. However, if she possessed the powers my mother described, she would probably see that coming.

After exchanging mean words, I decided to make the first move and bumped her with the same force I used on her mother in the office. My plan backfired as I lost my footing and struggled to regain balance. Shaylah swiftly grabbed hold of me, stopping a potentially bad fall down the stairs. I could have been really hurt.

Too proud to say thanks, I kept going up the stairs, annoyed that she helped me. Eventually, I made my way back to class.

Finally, the last bell rang, and I sprinted down the stairs, excited to be dismissed from school. Waiting on the steps for my mom to pick me up, an all-black Cadillac SUV pulled up. Inside sat a man and a woman I had never seen before.

The back window rolled down, revealing my mom. "Get in the car," she commanded, gesturing for me to join her in the back seat.

"Momma, who are these people?" I asked cautiously, my hand resting on the car door.

"This is Barbara and Maxwell. Now, hurry up and get in before someone sees us," my mother urged, a sense of urgency in her voice.

Hustling into the car, I sat beside my mother in the backseat, wondering why she was with these people.

We started a silent trip toward the inner city, the weight of uncertainty hanging in the air. As we pulled up to the curb across from Karma Plaza, we patiently awaited further instructions, our eyes fixed on the unfolding scene. My mom talked to the mysterious man and woman, but I lost interest. Could this be real?

And then, I spotted Shaylah emerging from the furniture shop, cradling a rectangular object wrapped in paper. "Momma, that's her. That's Shaylah right there," I said, pointing in Shaylah's direction.

"Are you sure she's the one with the pouch bearing the sign?" the woman in the front seat inquired.

"Yes, and her mother is trailing closely behind her. She came to pick her up early from school," I confirmed.

Barbara and Maxwell exchanged glances before speeding away, heading for our home.

My mother seemed uneasy, a level of agitation I had never seen before. When we got to our house, the woman in the front seat turned to look at us in the back.

"Geneva and Geni, wait for my instructions. You two are now activated. Shaylah must be eliminated before she unlocks the secrets of her powers and learns to control the roots. We must find the crystals before she realizes the extent of her true abilities. Your mother has done an exceptional job training you, Geni. Well done. Now, it's time to finish the task," Barbara commanded, her gaze stern and unwavering.

Roots? What roots?

My mother unlocked the car door, and we stepped out, ensuring we left no trace behind. As we walked toward the front door, I reached out and grabbed my mother's arm, halting her in her tracks. "Momma, wait. Who was that woman? I have never seen her before in my life. Where did she come from? And why do we have to kill Shaylah? What about the roots?"

"Slow down, Geni. I understand you have questions, and rightly so. First and foremost, Barbara and Maxwell are from Marston. They are Parjeks, hailing from the planet Parjeka," my mother explained as we entered the house and closed the door, our conversation shielded from prying ears.

"They are here to assist me in avenging the deaths of your father and grandfather."

We settled onto the couch in the living room, my mom was ready to handle business, while I was just looking for some answers.

"Shaylah's grandfather, RaKem, is held captive in Charcantium by the Parjeks. He remains unaware that we have discovered his descendants here on earth. We have been awaiting the revelation of the Darkest Light, and now the time has come. Shaylah herself embodies the Darkest Light. Once she masters her powers, she will command the rogue roots and with that power, rule over this realm."

"Wait, so I have to kill her? Why must we resort to such drastic measures? Can't we just take her powers and control the roots?" I questioned my unease growing at the thought of taking Shaylah's life. My animosity toward Shaylah at school was one thing, but actual murder was an entirely different realm.

"We cannot simply take her powers. In order for her to harness them, she must employ the Marston crystals. Only then can she wield her abilities. The descendant of the Darkest Light alone possesses the power to manipulate the energy within those stones and control the roots. To anyone else, they are nothing more than useless rocks. The roots lie buried beneath the surface in Marston, and with their power, we can seek vengeance for your grandfather's and father's deaths. No single individual should possess such overwhelming power. Shaylah must be eliminated. Anyone who stands in our way will meet the same fate. They have done a commendable job protecting her thus far, and they will continue to do everything in their power to shield her. The Marston's reign over the roots is drawing to a close. It is time for us to establish our legacy and claim their powers. We will ensure it. We will exterminate them all."

Standing up, my mother moved toward the fireplace mantle, delicately picking up Grandpapa's picture before gently placing it back down. As tears streamed down her face, she kissed Daddy's picture frame.

"Mom, I still don't understand. Is there no other way? Can't we find an alternative solution? I may despise Shaylah, but I don't want blood on my hands."

Who is this woman? This is not the mother I know.

Chapter 8

Shaylah

The car ride home after the incident was a mix of relief and apprehension. Momma and I shared a deep conversation, our voices mingling with laughter and concern. I recounted the terrifying moments in the bathroom, confessing how fear had reduced me to tears. Yet, as we delved deeper into the discussion, the tone grew serious, and Momma's questions became more probing.

"Was the bathroom empty, Shay? Did you follow the instructions exactly as I wrote them? Did you make sure not to leave anything behind?" Momma's voice brimmed with a mother's protective instinct.

My confession about it being a false alarm seemed to put Momma at ease. That was until I mentioned dropping the pouch. The encounter with Geni left Momma visibly shaken. She slammed on the brakes, bringing the car to an abrupt halt, and her cringed expression mirrored her concern.

"Shay, are you absolutely sure Geni didn't open it?" she asked, her voice tinged with anxiety.

"Yes, Momma, I'm certain. Those strings didn't budge," I reassured her, hoping to ease her worry.

Momma let out a sigh, staring straight ahead at the road, lost in her own thoughts. The weight of unsaid things hung heavy in the silence that wrapped around us for the rest of the ride, until we pulled up to Daddy's store, Mike's Woodworks.

"There are things that will soon make sense to you. But for now, as your mother, it's my duty to keep you safe. You are a special young lady, and you must never forget that," she assured me, her words wrapping me up in warmth and love. "First, we have to drop off your father's lunch, and then we'll visit Grandma Caly Rose. She has something for you, something she won't even reveal to me. She is going to help your father and I explain what is happening."

Stepping into the store, I was greeted by the familiar sight of Daddy's masterful creations. His craftsmanship was renowned, and people from far and wide sought out his unique and handmade furniture. Tall and athletically built, Daddy's presence commanded attention. His dark, shaved head gleamed as if kissed by the sun, while his full lips revealed a row of perfectly aligned, pearly white teeth. Almond-shaped eyes, slanted and expressive, framed a unique birthmark that adorned the right side of his eye and forehead—a mark he considered special, one that seemed to diminish in size as his eyes softened into a warm smile.

I couldn't help but feel a mixture of embarrassment and affectionate amusement as Daddy greeted Momma with a kiss that spoke of a love that hadn't faded since the morning. "Look at two of my favorite girls!" he exclaimed, his eyes shifting to meet mine. His smile widened, and his gaze lingered, brimming with so much love.

"Um, I'm right here, you know," I jumped in, feeling a little embarrassed by my parents' playful display.

"I'm sorry, Shay. Your mom is so breathtakingly beautiful that I had to kiss her, just to make sure I wasn't dreaming," Daddy said, his gaze fixed on her as he spoke.

"Michael, you're not too shabby-looking yourself. You're fine, fine," Momma replied shyly, her cheeks tinged with a rosy blush.

Momma handed Daddy the lunch she prepared for him, emphasizing the need to return the storage containers. He explained Grandma Caly Rose made a special request for the tray today, leading him to prioritize it above all his other orders. He asked us to personally deliver it to Grandma Caly Rose, making sure she received it. With a quick goodbye, he sent us off since he had to get back to his work.

Next to Daddy's store stood the Ground Source Healing Center, a place I had visited countless times before. I was welcomed by two majestic amethyst cathedrals, standing tall at ten feet in height, giving off an incredible burst of energy. Happiness coursed through me, embracing my being as I absorbed the vibrant sensation. It was an unfamiliar feeling this time around, strange yet undeniably pleasant. Pausing before the cathedrals, I felt as though I were seeing them for the first time, their imposing presence captivating my senses. The store itself seemed imbued with life, pulsating with an energy that enveloped me, offering comfort and solace.

Stepping into the store, I observed the walls painted in a deep purple hue. But this time, they seemed to sparkle like purple diamonds, casting a mesmerizing glow that illuminated the entire space. The floor beneath my feet felt solid and grounded, as if I were rooted deep within the earth. It provided me with a sense of stability and connection. The wall art, once dormant, now came alive, shimmering as if it had just been polished. The centerpiece of the room, the immense copper singing bowl, emitted a resonant and harmonious sound that resonated in my soul. Hovering above it, the large quartz crystal cluster radiated a powerful energy that suffused the entire space with a healing aura.

My gaze turned to Grandma Caly Rose, seated in her customary spot, spinning what I had always assumed was yarn. But this time, it appeared as if she were weaving strands of molten copper, a thin, shiny thread spiraling around the spool. She sat there, a vision of beauty, her skin glowing like my momma's had earlier in the day. Her chocolate complexion possessed a silky smoothness, reminiscent of a cacao bean. Jet-black hair flowed without a hint of gray, framing high cheekbones and a chiseled jawline. Pride radiated from her as she observed me, taking in the vibrant energy that imbued the store.

"That's right. Take it all in, my beautiful granddaughter," Grandma Caly Rose encouraged me, her voice gentle yet resonant. "This is a moment of great significance, one that fills me with immense pride. Moonia, please make sure to close and lock the door," she instructed Momma, pausing her spinning to embrace me with a hug and a kiss on the cheek.

Without hesitation, Momma secured the glass double doors, flipping the sign to indicate the store was closed. One by one, she drew the thick deep purple curtains, veiling the room in darkness until only the skylight above the suspended crystal remained, casting its ethereal light upon us.

Using the radiant glow of the room as her guide, Momma made her way to the kitchenette, preparing Grandma Caly Rose's favorite tea. The aroma wafted through the air, mingling with the ambiance of the space, an olfactory symphony of fragrant notes.

Grandma Caly Rose turned her attention to me, gesturing for me to bring the Moroccan pouf ottoman made of leather, sewn together with her shimmering copper yarn. She was a spiritual metaphysical healer, or at least that's what she told me.

"Moonia, is the tea ready?" Grandma Caly Rose asked Momma, her voice a blend of urgency and playfulness. "I'm eager to commence the ritual."

Ritual. What ritual?

"I thank your father and mother for granting me the permission to show you who you are. To tell you everything you must know," Grandma Caly Rose declared.

Confusion and excitement swirled within me as Grandma Caly Rose approached the table, cradling a round black crystal sphere that never before graced my sight. Placing it atop an intricately carved wooden base, shaped like winding roots, Grandma Caly Rose evoked a sense of ancient wisdom and mystical connection. I found myself captivated, losing myself in the intricacies of the carving, unable to discern where it began and where it ended.

With grace and purpose, Momma unwrapped the wooden tray Daddy handed us earlier. It was a rectangle tray crafted from petrified wood, adorned with delicate copper filigree handles on each side. Upon the tray, a crystal box, bundles of fragrant white sage from Grandma Caly Rose's garden, a canister of her beloved quartz crystal tea, three small copper tea cups, a gleaming copper tea kettle filled with steaming water, and a magnificent amethyst crystal cluster found their places. The air carried the enchanting scent of frankincense incense, as Momma lit a charcoal tablet and placed three small morsels on it, releasing wisps of fragrant smoke that swirled and twirled.

Across the table, Grandma Caly Rose ignited a purple candle, its flickering flame a mesmerizing dance of light and shadow. The candle seemed to hold within it a kaleidoscope of herbs and sparkling glitter, casting a soft, mystical glow upon the room.

In a deliberate and unusual gesture, Grandma Caly Rose, typically a left-handed woman, held her teacup in her right hand, a deviation from her usual habits. With focused attention, she poured the hot water into her cup, watching intently as the leaves transformed, unfurling and infusing the water with their essence.

Eyes closed, Grandma Caly Rose began to chant, her voice a melodic incantation that reverberated through the room. "I, Caly Rose Marston, wife of the great RaKem Marston, stand before you, my glorious and benevolent ancestors. Together with Shaylah Marston, heir to the Darkest Light of RaKem Marston, we invoke your presence. As Jewel descendants of Marston, we call upon you to open the gate, synchronize the three corners of her sacred body, and bestow upon her the power of the Marston crystal. Shaylah Marston, granddaughter of the mighty RaKem, is prepared to receive your ancient knowledge, infinite wisdom, and boundless powers from our ancestral land. Mighty ancestors, protect her from harm, guide her on her path, and grant her communion with the spirit of the rogue roots. Guard and honor her as the Darkest Light."

With each word, Grandma Caly Rose's voice grew in intensity, carrying the weight of generations past. Momma, too, joined in the chant, her voice seamlessly blending with Grandma Caly Rose's, becoming a unified force.

And then, as if the universe itself responded to their call, something extraordinary occurred. The purple gem embedded in the center of my bracelet began to radiate, casting a captivating glow that enveloped us all. In this moment, we saw the coming together of energies, the alignment of destinies.

Grandma Caly Rose raised her hands toward the heavens, a gesture of reverence and acknowledgment. "They are with us, Shaylah. Can you feel the spirits of the roots? They are listening, ready to heed your commands.

Embrace this moment, for it marks the threshold of your extraordinary journey," Grandma Caly Rose conveyed, her eyes gleaming with pride and anticipation.

Caught between confusion and excitement, I looked to Momma and Grandma Caly Rose, searching their expressions for answers. The weight of my recent experiences pressed upon me, and the revelation of a hidden world left me longing for understanding.

"Could someone please explain what is happening already?" I implored, my frustration mingling with genuine curiosity. "From the strange dream this morning, to the strategic list of instructions to the abrupt early pickup from school, and now this ritual. I was just here yesterday, and the store was worn and dusty. No offense, Grandma Caly Rose," I added hastily, voicing my perplexity and impatience.

"Mind your tone, young lady," Grandma Caly Rose commanded firmly, her voice carrying a gentle reprimand.

With determined strides, Grandma Caly Rose approached the magnificent copper singing bowl, its presence now revealed as an instrument of ethereal power. Walking around the bowl, she created a symphony of celestial tones that filled the room, surpassing even the enchanting melody that greeted me upon entering.

"Perhaps we should reconsider, Momma Caly Rose. Shaylah may not be ready for this just yet," my mom suggested, her voice laced with concern as she walked toward Grandma Caly Rose, offering her the rectangular box.

"Nonsense, Moonia. The gate hummed the moment she crossed its threshold. If it stirs, then the time is ripe," Grandma Caly Rose declared, undeterred.

She continued her measured steps, encircling the singing bowl with purpose. And in a breathtaking instant, the massive quartz crystal suspended above the bowl emitted a beam of luminosity so brilliant that it pierced the very heart of the vessel, revealing a concealed passageway beyond.

Chapter 9

Caly Rose

Shaylah stood frozen, her body rigid with shock. Moonia wrapped her arms around Shaylah, holding her face gently. "Shay, everything will be alright. I'm here with you. Believe it or not, this is the safest place on the entire planet. You'll see soon enough," Moonia reassured her.

As we approached the copper singing bowl, Shaylah and Moonia following closely behind me, I couldn't help but think this must be one of those surreal dreams where portals open up. But no, this was real, and I wasn't going to let this opportunity slip away. It was happening and happening fast. So I pinched myself hard on my hand, uttering a soft, "Ouch."

"Are you alright?" Moonia asked, halting me in my tracks.

"Yes, I'm fine, Moonia," I replied.

We guided Shaylah to stand inside the singing bowl, positioned on a magnificent spiral staircase.

"What in the world is this place? And how long have you both been keeping it from me?" Shaylah asked, her curiosity piqued.

"Come on inside, dear. We don't have much time. I have a patient to see in an hour," I urged Shaylah, guiding her toward the staircase.

Approaching the opening of the copper singing bowl, I joined Shaylah and Moonia on the staircase. The stairs glistened like polished black glass. The copper railing sparkled, adorned with quartz crystal bars along its entire length, creating a grand and captivating sight.

As we descended the staircase, my gaze shifted upward, marveling at the majestic quartz crystal positioned above the copper singing bowl in the store. Its beauty seemed even more mesmerizing from this vantage point. I paused at the bottom of the staircase, awestruck by what lay before me.

"These three colossal doors are crafted from pure twenty-four karat gold!" I exclaimed, standing in admiration of their dazzling sparkle. "This central door leads to the River Room. We'll explore the other two doors on another day."

Taking deliberate steps toward the door, the intricate labyrinthine lock moved as I waved my hand counterclockwise in front of it. It was no ordinary lock, possessing multiple maze-like layers that would baffle an untrained person attempting to unravel it. I began chanting, "I, Caly Rose Marston, wife of RaKem Marston, stand before you with the Darkest Light, Shaylah Marston. She is now activated. With your blessing, grant us safe passage," I declared, gently touching the lock.

Standing before the door with one hand resting on my hip and my head tilted slightly to the side, I hoped I hadn't missed any crucial part of the chant. Impatience welled up inside me. Suddenly, the lock began to unravel, layer by meticulous layer. The heavy door slowly swung open. I reached out to join hands with Shaylah, while Moonia grasped my hand tightly, and together we stepped through the door, flanked by two majestic golden pillars that towered toward the vaulted ceiling.

"How can we be passing through a door with such a high ceiling? Aren't we in the basement?" Shaylah asked, her curiosity piqued.

"Let's find a comfortable spot to sit," I suggested, leading Moonia and Shaylah to a cozy nook next to a gleaming Olympic-sized pool at the center of the room. The water shimmered and danced, reminiscent of the waters of Charcantium, my home planet.

"You mean to tell me that on those scorching ozone days, we could have been swimming down here? That's unbelievable, keeping this magnificent pool all to yourselves," Shaylah remarked, gazing admiringly at the water.

"Shay, there is so much we need to tell you about who you are. You are an extraordinary young lady," I explained.

"You were born in these very waters. I have never seen water move and dance the way it did on the night of your birth. The water remembers you," Moonia added.

"You are a gift from the universe. Words cannot express the joy that fills me today. Right now, at this very moment, anything is possible. It is time I reveal to you who you are and why this day is so significant to all of us," I proclaimed.

Shaylah's eyes widened, a mix of anticipation and disbelief washing over her. "I know, I know. I'm a very special young lady. But what is it? What is it about me, Grandma Caly Rose? What else do I need to know?"

I placed my hands gently onto Shaylah's shoulders, along with a reassuring smile on my face. "You have been blessed by the creators with abilities so powerful, only you can contain and control them. As a witness to these powers, the same power that your grandfather had, I'm here to guide you. I will help you unlock your abilities, discover your true potential to navigate the challenges that lie ahead. But the choice ultimately rests with you. It is your journey, your destiny," I explained, hoping Shaylah understood the magnitude of what this meant for her.

I took a deep breath, my emotions swirled within me. I looked around, shifting my attention from Shaylah to the shimmering water screen, displaying images of Charcantium.

In that moment, Shaylah made her decision, captivated by the magic unfolding before her eyes. "I want to embrace my destiny. I want to learn and understand who I truly am," Shaylah declared, determination resonating in her voice.

Moonia and I exchanged proud smiles, a profound sense of hope and purpose filling the air.

"Then let the journey begin," I said, my voice carrying a weight of purpose. And with those words, Moonia and I walked up alongside Shaylah.

"Allow me to acquaint you with the profound significance of this day and reveal the essence of your being," I said to Shaylah. "The time has come for us to unravel the tale that will explain everything."

Feeling the weight of anticipation in my words, I called out to the water, my voice filled with an unwavering determination. "Guide me back to our cherished abode. Take us to Charcantium."

As if responding to my plea, the water began to transform, assuming the form of a colossal rectangular screen, suspended in the air like a grand theater display. It swirled and contorted, molding itself into a smooth surface, upon which the images of my beloved home began to materialize.

"In the beginning, when our planet, Charcantium, was born, the galaxy boasted but a meager handful of dimly lit stars. Our home was a breathtaking paradise, adorned with shimmering lakes and rivers that flowed with a weightless elegance. The very water that now mirrored before us held the essence of those ethereal streams.

"Charcantium was inhabited by two distinct peoples, who coexisted harmoniously. The Beholders were renowned for their gifts of healing, and the Master Beholder safeguarded the revered Tetratetum—a sacred artifact. On the other hand, the Jewels, descendants of royalty from an ancient galaxy, possessed the extraordinary ability to birth the Darkest Light, an individual capable of controlling the roots by harnessing the boundless power within the Charcantium crystals housed within the Tetratetum. Only the Darkest Light held the ability to transfer this infinite wellspring of energy, thereby maintaining the equilibrium and serenity of our realm.

"Every sixty years, the incumbent Darkest Light would embark upon Mt. Charcantium, a treacherous journey that unveiled the successor to the throne. This momentous occasion was celebrated with jubilant festivities, featuring an abundance of food, dancing, craftsmanship, and games, embodying the very essence of balance and peace of our people. Visitors from far-flung reaches of the universe would traverse unfathomable distances to witness this extraordinary event, to experience the revelation of the chosen one.

"Throughout the existence of Charcantium, many visitors graced our planet's shores, incoming and departing in harmony. However, the arrival of the Parjeks shattered this idyllic tranquility. Hailing from Parjeka, a planet situated two light years away from our illustrious Charcantium star, they descended upon us

unannounced. Their intrusion disrupted the sacred invocation. Outsiders could bear witness to the event yet were forbidden from partaking in the rituals. They did not simply wish to observe but wanted to take part in our sacred practices and become one with us. The Parjeks shared tales of their home world's decimation at the hands of the Bandrala, urging us to take heed of the formidable army that plundered their resources and enslaved their people. Driven by a desperate desire to safeguard their kin, they sought refuge on Charcantium, hoping to find the means to defend their own.

"Your grandfather, RaKem, did not extend a warm welcome to the Parjeks, and with good reason. He sensed the palpable difference in their energy, a stark contrast to the essence cherished by the people of Charcantium. He demanded their swift departure. In due course, a momentous council meeting commenced, where leaders from both families convened to determine whether the Parjeks' would be permitted to refuge. The Jewels and RaKem voted against their stay, while the Beholders, along with their kin, favored extending an invitation.

"Our civilized system allowed the Parjeks to remain on Charcantium, on the condition that they assimilate into our way of life and actively contribute to every facet of our peaceful and balanced society. And so, without delay, the Parjeks embraced our guiding principles, adopting our unified ways of peace and cooperative economic strategies as their highest priority.

"With the assimilation of the Parjeks complete, the invocation of the Darkest Light could resume after one year.

"The fateful evening arrived, signaling the commencement of the odyssey. RaKem and the Master Beholder embarked on the perilous journey through the realms of the past, present, and the fifth dimension to seek out the next heir within the lineage of Jewels.

"Prior to RaKem's departure, he bestowed a tender kiss upon the foreheads of our slumbering twin daughters, Vania and Denise, and gently patted his son Ellbey's head. His eyes then met mine, with a silent plea for understanding.

"'Ra, I ask that you return back to us swiftly. Our baby could arrive at any moment. Could you not allow the Master Beholder to undertake this journey alone, just this once?' I pleaded, desperately clinging to hope.

"'Rosie, you know interfering with destiny is not our path. I shall return before you even realize I am gone,' RaKem reassured me, attempting to put an end to my fears before his departure.

"That night, under the cover of darkness, RaKem and the Master Beholder embarked upon their quest. Their destination was not far, a mere three-hour trek through the lush Charcantium forest. It led them to the apex of Mt. Charcantium, where the portal to the past, present, and the fifth dimension awaited.

"'I, RaKem Marston, the Darkest Light, beseech the portal to the past, present, and the fifth dimension. Reveal to me the descendant destined to be the Supreme Ruler of Charcantium. Show me the Darkest Light, who shall command the rogue roots,' RaKem proclaimed with unyielding resolve.

"The Master Beholder handed RaKem the revered Tetratetum, an intricate box that held profound significance. RaKem, holding the sacred artifact aloft, sought permission and blessings from the ancestors to access the portal. The box, adorned with a labyrinthine copper lock, came alive, its intricate design unfurling to grant RaKem access. Opening the box, he retrieved the three luminous Charcantium crystals nestled within. Gently closing the box, he returned it to the Master Beholder. With a clenched fist, RaKem struck the ground with one hand, and held the crystals toward the sky with the other. The earth quaked beneath his feet, carving deep furrows into the verdant grass. From the depths of the soil, thick, glossy, reddish-brown roots erupted, encircling RaKem and lifting him skyward. He reverently caressed the roots as they gently lowered him back to the ground, leading him to the portal where a radiant beam of white light rotated before him. The portal expanded, pulsating with blinding brilliance, as hazy images of a room gradually crystallized within.

"RaKem peered into the portal, casting his gaze upon the past, present, and the fifth dimension, into the confines of Michael and Moonia's bedroom, while Shaylah lay nestled in her crib.

"'That is a splendid crib, young man,' he murmured, stepping through the portal. The room shimmered and stretched as he advanced. The roots, faithful to their purpose, followed RaKem, tenderly brushing against Shaylah's cheek before parting into two, swirling around the crib's frame. RaKem strolled around the crib, marveling at Michael's handiwork, running his hand along the length of the Charcantium-inspired structure. The petrified wood frame gave it a royal look.

The bars, made from quartz crystal, looked like they had a magical glow. Even the screws that held it all together were made from super special rock called hematite. To make it even better, the crib was covered in the softest cotton bedding.

"As RaKem approached Shaylah's crib, a smile graced his countenance, his eyes alight with affection. At that moment, Shaylah stirred, raising the right side of her plump cheek, revealing tiny, pink gums and offering a radiant smile. RaKem's admiration paused briefly as the roots settled around the crib, rousing Shaylah from her slumber. The gentle settling sound caused Michael and Moonia to shift in their beds, but they remained immersed in their sleep.

"RaKem took a few moments to cast his gaze upon Michael and Moonia, observing their peaceful repose. However, his expression shifted to one of concern as he approached their bedside. With utmost care, he leaned in, studying Michael's face, his attention drawn to the deep, swollen gash beneath his eye, and then to the red, raised welt adorning Moonia's cheek. A profound worry furrowed his brow.

"Softly, he reached out, his touch gliding over Michael's cheek, a miraculous healing energy flowing from his fingertips, mending the wound on his face. Moonia's welt, too, swiftly succumbed to the healing touch, vanishing within seconds. RaKem's gaze then shifted to the dresser, where he lifted a photograph of me, a fond smile gracing his lips. 'I love you, Rosie,' he whispered, as if I could hear his words.

"The past, present, and the fifth dimension began to close, the portal receding a few steps away from RaKem. He redirected his attention to Shaylah, who observed him silently, her eyes fixed upon his form. With tiny hands, she reached out, grasping his finger, eliciting a warm smile from him. Leaning down, he tenderly pressed his forehead against hers, a silent telepathic message passing between the two.

"'I am your grandpa, little one. You are the heir to the throne, destined to return to Charcantium and claim your rightful place as the Darkest Light—the one and only Supreme Ruler capable of harnessing the true power of the Charcantium crystals and controlling the rogue roots,' he conveyed, his voice resounding in the depths of Shaylah's consciousness.

"In an unforeseen burst of chaos, an explosion rocked the room, hurtling two Parjeks through the portal, accompanied by smoldering roots that cascaded into

Shaylah's crib. RaKem, ever vigilant, engaged one of the Parjeks in battle, while the other seized Shaylah by the feet, swinging her through the portal's opening. Shaylah landed atop the Master Beholder, who lay upon the ground, clinging to life by a fragile thread. With his last reserves of strength, he cradled Shaylah in his arms as she cried.

"'So, you are the future,' he uttered, his voice tinged with both awe and melancholy. And then, his arm fell limply to the side.

"RaKem emerged from the hazy, glowing portal, dragging the disarmed and captured Parjeks with him. Urgently, he rushed to the side of the fallen Master Beholder, Shaylah's wailing form cradled gently against his chest. He hurriedly returned Shaylah to the safety of her crib, careful not to disturb Michael and Moonia. Yet, Shaylah's pout and cries persisted. Just as RaKem passed back through the portal to Mt. Charcantium, Michael stirred, awakening to Shaylah's tearful distress."

Chapter 10

Caly Rose

"The summit of Mt. Charcantium was a scene of utter chaos, the air thick with disbelief and confusion. Onlookers gathered, their expressions a mix of shock and sorrow, as they surrounded the lifeless body of the Master Beholder. A crowd slowly formed around his body. Their murmurs blending into a somber symphony of grief.

"Genelle, the Master Beholder's wife, let out a piercing cry of anguish, her sorrow reverberating through the crowd. 'They killed him!' she wailed, her voice choked with pain. 'They've taken everything from us. Michael...our children...RaKem, how could you let this happen?' Her voice trailing off, consumed by the weight of her grief.

"Tears steadily streamed down her face as she cradled the spirit orb of her beloved husband, a radiant sphere of light that had departed his lifeless body. She tenderly placed it around her neck, the orb serving as a haunting reminder of her loss. RaKem embraced Genelle, hurt by the loss of his friend.

"'Genelle, I'm so sorry. We were attacked by Parjeks and they killed Michael while I was inside the portal,' RaKem explained. 'Right now, we must head back to town to rid our planet of these evil beings.'

"RaKem led the grief-stricken Beholders and Jewels down the slopes of the mountain, each step heavy with sorrow. Emmerson, RaKem's younger brother, approached him, his voice laced with concern.

"'Brother, what has transpired? Is it true? Is Michael truly gone?'

"RaKem's voice carried a profound sadness as he confirmed the devastating news. 'Yes, it is true. The Parjeks attacked us, and Michael...he did not survive. They followed us through the portal and ambushed us. Their betrayal runs deep.'

"Emmerson's voice trembled with anger and desperation. 'The Parjeks have turned against us. Our land is ravaged, our people suffering. They poisoned our mules, destroyed our crops, and chained our kin like beasts. Our very existence is under threat. Why haven't the rogue roots been summoned to protect us?'

"RaKem's gaze grew distant, his thoughts wandering to the realm of prophecy. 'You know I cannot interfere with destiny. Calling upon the rogue roots would bring about the end of Charcantium, the extinction of the Darkest Light. We must trust the process, as difficult as it may be.'

"Emmerson's brow furrowed, his voice tinged with uncertainty. 'But how will we know? How will we find our way through this darkness?'

"RaKem's eyes met his brother's, a flicker of resolve shining within them. 'The signs will reveal themselves, Emmerson. We must remain vigilant and have faith. Trust the process. The next Darkest Light was revealed. Summoning the roots now would lead the Parjeks right to her.'

"'Her?'

"'Yes her, Emmerson. Now, I must find Rosie.'

"With a mix of calm and uncertainty, RaKem reassured Emmerson, knowing the path forward was shrouded in uncertainty now that the Master Beholder was dead and the Parjeks turned on the Chacantium people.

"As RaKem retraced his steps, his mind wandered to the Tetratetum and the crystals it held. Fumbling through his pockets, he found only two of the three precious gems. He realized that the third crystal had been lost during the altercation with the Parjeks in the portal. Regret washed over him momentarily, but he knew there was no turning back. With care, he placed the remaining crystals inside the Tetratetum, closing it with a sense of finality.

"'Rosie, I have returned,' RaKem called out to me cautiously, standing before the now-empty threshold of our home.

"Broken glass littered the floor, furnishings lay in disarray, and torn paintings decorated the walls. Stepping outside, RaKem and Emmerson encountered a neighbor, his wounded arm being tended to.

"'They've taken them, RaKem,' the neighbor informed them, a sense of urgency in his voice. 'Caly Rose is in grave danger. They have your children and they threatened to harm them all if you don't hand over the Charcantium crystals.'

"Thanking the neighbor for his bravery, RaKem's determination solidified. He instructed Emmerson to stay behind to rally all able-bodied men to prepare for war and set off toward the woods, following a Parjek guardsman, his resolve unwavering. With a well-executed diversion, RaKem subdued the guard, quietly subduing him to avoid drawing attention to their location. Disguising himself in the guard's clothes, RaKem made his way to an old, abandoned shack hidden deep within the forest.

"The second Parjek barely noticed RaKem's impersonation, and the third, the largest of them all, soon became suspicious.

"'State your allegiance,' the Parjek guard demanded.

"Cover blown, with swift and precise movements, RaKem defended himself against the Parjek's assault, his skill evident as he deflected blows and unleashed counterattacks. The clash ended in a fatal exchange, ending with the three Parjeks lifeless bodies crumpling to the ground.

"Inside the shack, I cried out for help, praying for someone to rescue me from my tormentors. The cacophony of the struggle outside slowly receded, replaced by careful footsteps approaching the door. RaKem wasted no time, forcefully kicking down the door to free me from my captivity.

"I sobbed uncontrollably, my hands cradling my protruding pregnant belly, anguish etched on my face. RaKem gently removed the shackles that marred my wrists, his touch tender and filled with love healing the deep bloody welts left behind. I shared with him the horrors I had endured, how the Parjeks had torn our family apart, their nefarious plans to harness the power of the Charcantium crystals and control the rogue roots.

"RaKem held me tightly in his arms, comforting and assuring me. 'We will not let them succeed, Rosie. There is another way,' he murmured, his voice filled with determination. He paced the confines of the shack, his mind burdened with the knowledge he gained from the past-present fifth dimension.

"'Quickly, come with me. I will open the portal. It is our only chance to save our legacy,' RaKem urged, his thoughts heavy with the weight of their decision.

"Torn between uncertainty and love, I pleaded with him to take our children and we escape together. But RaKem had already made up his mind, his resolve unyielding. With tearful farewells and whispered promises, he handed me a small neatly engraved leather satchel, its contents a mystery.

"'Where will it take me?' I asked, stepping into the capsule, my heart pounding with both fear and hope. But before his words reached my ears, I was thrust backward against the wall, the force of the capsule propelling me forward, away from Charcantium and into a new world."

Chapter 11

Caly Rose

"Inside the capsule, a wave of excitement coursed through my veins. The air crackled with electric energy, charged by the promise of adventure. RaKem quickly closed the door and I sealed the hatch shut with a resolute click, enclosing myself in a cocoon of safety amid the chaos that awaited. My heart raced in rhythm with the thrumming vibrations resonating through the capsule's metallic walls, as if heralding the imminent descent into the uncharted depths of the unknown. In synchrony, we touched the window to the capsule and RaKem signaled it to enter the portal.

"The moment of departure arrived, there was no turning back. With a deafening roar, the capsule hurtled downward, piercing through the veil of reality and the portal. A whirlwind of emotions swirled within me. I was filled with exhilaration, trepidation, and wonder.

"The atmospheric pressure intensified, squeezing my eardrums as the rushing wind enveloped the capsule, buffeting it with unseen forces. The world outside transformed into a kaleidoscope of colors and shapes, a fleeting mosaic of ever-changing beauty. My body was violently jolted in every direction, pressed forcefully against the walls of the capsule. Within the confines, a symphony of blinding white iridescent lights danced and swirled, captivating me in an ethereal embrace. Rays of vibrant hues, woven with mystical energy, painted the walls with pulsating *luminescence, creating an otherworldly panorama resembling swollen veins pumping with life. Their presence spoke of unseen realms and hidden truths, igniting a sense of wonder in my heart as a lone voyager.*

"Amid the kaleidoscope of luminosity, a core brilliance emerged—a beacon of resplendent white light. It radiated an aura of pure enchantment, unmatched by any celestial body. It bathed the capsule in a soft, ethereal glow, imbuing the air with an otherworldly serenity.

"The space capsule became a sanctuary—my protection within the portal into realms unknown, an ark carrying my hopes, dreams, and my family's future.

"As I gazed upon the symphony, a sense of awe and reverence swelled within my chest. The blinding lights evoked a primal connection, filling my heart with gratitude and a resolute determination to venture forth into the uncharted abyss of the cosmos.

"Dread gripped my heart, intertwining with the fierce ache in my belly, as I clung to the precious life growing within. With every fiber of my being, I yearned for both my unborn child and I to withstand the tumultuous voyage that lay ahead. A second portal, a gateway to unknown worlds, loomed before me, emanating an aura of profound mystery.

"Suddenly, a breathtaking vista came into view, an expansive body of water shimmering beneath the luminescent sky. It was in this fleeting moment of desperation that instinct took hold, and I made a split-second decision. With a flick of a lever, I released the burning shell of the capsule, casting it over the watery expanse, hoping to confuse the relentless assault of the flying objects pursuing me. Flames danced in the air, an infernal display of chaos, as the exterior of the capsule reached critical capacity, its fiery embrace threatening to consume it entirely.

"Inside the safety of the capsule, I braced myself for the inevitable impact. The ground rushed up to meet me with a bone-rattling force. The towering trees of the densely wooded area loomed closer, their ancient branches reaching out as if to catch me in their gnarled embrace. Twisted roots tangled beneath the forest floor, the earth shaking with the weight of the crash landing. The capsule skidded and jolted, its metallic frame protesting against the unyielding terrain, before finally coming to a shuddering halt.

"Silence settled over the wreckage, broken only by my labored breaths and the

crackling of the dying flames that licked at the outer hull. A haze of smoke hung heavy in the air, mingling with the scent of charred wood and foliage. I pressed a hand to my pounding heart, my body trembling with the aftershocks of the harrowing descent.

"Finally, my body peeled away from the capsule wall, and I was flung into a thorny shrub bush. Landing awkwardly, my hands and knees met the stiff, piercing thorns of green shrubs. Numbness crept over my punctured skin as I painstakingly removed each thorn, slightly pinching the wounds to encourage swelling and stem the bleeding. The thorns had woven themselves into my royal garb, and I carefully tore away the top layer, leaving it behind.

"With no time to spare, I retracted back to the damaged capsule, my nerves on edge with every cautious step.

"'This capsule will self-destruct in thirty seconds. Thirty. Twenty-nine. Twenty-eight,' a mechanical voice echoed through the fading capsule.

"I swiftly gathered the satchel and made my hasty exit. Using a piece of cloth from my dress, I fashioned a weapon by tightly wrapping a sharp metal shard salvaged from the capsule for protection.

"The atmosphere of this unknown world embraced me like a long lost relative. The air crackled with an electric charge, humming with an otherworldly energy that seemed to permeate every molecule. The distant sounds of the forest came alive, a symphony of rustling leaves, chattering critters, and the haunting echoes of unseen creatures.

"As I surveyed my surroundings, I couldn't help but wonder aloud, 'Where am I?' Placing a hand protectively over my contracting belly, I took in the unfamiliar forest surrounding me. Towering pine trees stretched into the sky, their peaks obscured from view. I ripped the satin inner lining of my garb and tied back my yarn braids. Darkness was descending, and my instincts directed me southward.

"Embarking on my trek through the woods, worry and paranoia fueled every step I took in the initial miles. I brandished my knife in defense at every rustling sound that emanated from the underbrush. Gazing up at the dark blue sky adorned with countless shimmering stars, I whispered, 'I am safe, my love,' hoping somehow, RaKem could sense I was alright.

"As I continued my journey through the woods, my baby's movements intensified, resting heavily on my bladder. After forty-five minutes of walking, the twisting sensations in my stomach grew more pronounced, accompanied by a low growling noise. Hunger gripped me, and I realized my baby was hungry, too. Fatigue began to weigh me down.

"'Come on, Caly Rose. You can do this, girl,' I encouraged myself, deciding to take a momentary break. I sat down near a colossal, toppled tree, kicking off my flat sandals. Crafted from leather with carnelian and gold accents, they were a testament to the beauty of craftsmanship prevalent on Charcantium. I turned my gaze toward the night sky, seeking guidance from the North Star. It served as my compass as I stood again and continued my southward trek, hunger growing with each step.

"The earth's energy surged, becoming increasingly potent the farther I journeyed from the North Star. With the night deepening, I soon realized that wandering through the woods was not a viable option. I needed to find a safe place to rest, as well as food and water.

"Almost as if in response to my thoughts, I stumbled upon a small river. Cupping my hands, I dipped them into the chilly water, the sensation soothing the puncture wounds from the thorns and reviving my weary senses. Taking a quick sip, I noticed a secluded grove near the mouth of a cave in the distance.

"Gathering my belongings, I limped cautiously toward the grove, scanning the cave's interior for any signs of danger.

"Assured of its safety, I entered the cave, my body growing weaker with each step. Collapsing onto a patch of soft green grass, I leaned against the cave wall. Weary and fatigued, I closed my eyes and gradually surrendered to sleep.

"Sometime later, a warm droplet of liquid trickled down my forehead, rousing me from my slumber. My eyes flew open to the sight of a massive black bear looming over me. It emitted a low, hungry growl, causing my baby to twist inside my womb.

"This couldn't be happening now.

"Summoning the last remnants of strength, I positioned myself defensively, ready to confront the bear. Its cold, black eyes locked with mine, and its long tongue swept across its lips. Extending my left hand toward the cave's ceiling, the bear began to pace back-and-forth, slowly cornering me against the cave wall. Rising onto its hind legs, it emitted a deep, resonant bellowing growl. I tried to shuffle away, but I was already backed against the wall. Trapped, I faced the bear with my right hand outstretched. Our gazes locked, and in that moment, I silently pleaded for the bear to turn and leave.

"My body trembled uncontrollably as hot, salty tears streamed down my face. The ability to communicate with animals, my once trusted gift, had abandoned me. The bear's growls intensified, reverberating through the cave, inching closer with every step. Face to face, the bear's heated breath mingled with my tears.

"Closing my eyes, I delved deep into my memories, recalling moments spent with animals I cared for. Forehead pressed against forehead, my tears ceased abruptly. Was I dead? Fear gave way to a peculiar calmness as I felt the bear's soft fur brush against my hand. Startled, I opened my eyes and gingerly petted the bear, and to my surprise, it gently nudged my bulging belly. I sank against the cave wall, shaking from the death-defying moment and the chilling cold that permeated the air. With no energy left to protest, I allowed the bear to envelop my shivering body in its warm fur.

"That night, nestled against the black bear, I slept undisturbed and protected. The frigid cave, where the biting wind had previously tormented me, ceased to exist within the bear's embrace. Its heartbeat slowed to a steady, rhythmic pulse, and the bear adjusted its position, directing the warmth of its belly toward me. I lay comforted, trapped within a trance, focusing on my breathing as my consciousness sank deeper. Memories of my family, of RaKem, of Marston, flickered through my mind.

"In the depths of my peaceful slumber, I was abruptly awoken by the gnawing ache of hunger. The once vicious windstorm had relented during the night, allowing a sense of tranquility to settle upon the land. My baby stirred within me, tiny feet jabbing against my side. 'Calm down, little one,' I whispered, my voice laced with a comforting tone. 'We will find food soon.'

"As if responding to my words, the bear that had provided me shelter slowly uncurled from its protective embrace and gracefully made its way out of the cave. Gratitude welled within me, and I uttered a heartfelt thank you, even though the bear continued onward without so much as a backward glance.

"Seated upon the still-warm grass, I retrieved my pouch, assessing the meager supplies I managed to gather from the capsule. The sharp chard served its purpose, allowing me to cut small pieces of moss from the cave wall. The green moss, though cold, possessed a chewy texture and a bitter taste. Opening the pouch, I gazed upon one Charcantium crystal it safeguarded. Its radiant glow illuminated the dark recesses of the cave, casting an ethereal glow upon the surrounding walls. The crystal only revealed its luminescence in the presence of copper, its brilliance reflecting the specks of the precious metal scattered throughout the cave.

"A sudden snap of breaking branches jolted me from my thoughts, causing me to choke on the last morsel of moss I dug from the cave wall.

"'Who's there?' I called out, my voice laced with a tinge of aggression.

"Instinctively, I assumed a defensive posture, clapping my hands thrice. But to my relief, it was none other than my friend, the bear. My anxieties dissipated as she approached, bearing the fruits of her hunting prowess. Two freshly killed salmon lay before me, disgorged from her warm, slimy mouth. With a gentle nudge of her nose, she encouraged me to partake in the sustenance she provided."

"The idea of consuming raw, uncooked fish turned my stomach, but declining the bear's offering was not an option. So, with a deep breath, I grasped the fish with both hands, bending its belly toward me, and took a bite. A resounding crunch echoed in the air, signaling my acquiescence to the bear's gift. I chewed and chewed until the bear seemed content, finally indulging in the saliva-drenched fish in front of her. Taking advantage of the distraction, I discreetly spat out the chewed remnants and cleansed my palate by consuming the last morsel of moss."

"Seated beside the bear, my baby finally content and resting after our meal, I couldn't help but feel a sense of disorientation. I remained oblivious to our whereabouts, yet an undeniable force drew me away from the North Star, leading me on a path where the natural energy of the earth grew stronger with each passing step. I glanced at the bear, rising to my feet, my head slowly leaning in to touch her forehead. In that silent gesture, my gratitude was conveyed. The bear reciprocated, reaching up with her paw to gently pat my back in acknowledgment.

"'Alright, bear,' I began, my voice laden with a touch of weariness. 'I must continue on my journey.'

"As I walked toward the entrance of the cave, the bear brushed against me, causing a slight momentary loss of balance. It then knelt down, bowing gracefully, inviting me to climb onto its back. I obliged, settling myself atop the majestic creature.

"With the bear carrying me upon its back, we made our way alongside the pebbled stream. Birds serenaded us with their melodious songs, while the gurgling water whispered its harmonious notes as it wove its way along the winding path. The scenery unfolded in picturesque beauty, an enchanting tapestry of nature's splendor. Yet, amid the breathtaking surroundings, my heart longed for the familiar comforts of Charcantium. Homesickness tugged at my core, aching for the warmth of familiarity.

"After two hours of traversing the untamed wilderness, we arrived at the shore of a sandy, white beach. The water shimmered with the hue of the midday sky, its vibrant blue mirroring the heavens above. Not a soul was in sight, and as the cloak of darkness began to descend, I spied an abandoned kayak a few feet away. A bittersweet understanding passed between the bear and me, for we both knew that our time together had reached its end.

"'Thank you for all you've done,' I expressed, embracing the bear one final time.

"Pushing the kayak into the chilly waters of the vast blue lake, I used a makeshift paddle I found to propel myself toward the mysterious destination that awaited me on the other side. Nightfall was approaching, and the wind picked up, causing the once calm lake to churn with choppy waves. The kayak teetered precariously, threatening to tip me over as the storm raged on. Thunder boomed and lightning streaked across the darkened sky, engaged in an otherworldly dance.

"But I had not come this far just to perish here. Summoning all my remaining strength, I fought against the relentless current, struggling to keep my head above water and gasp for precious breaths of air. The storm's turbulence thrashed me about like a rag doll, while lightning crackled and thunder roared. The fish beneath me sought refuge in the depths, stunned by the electrified waters. Yet, miraculously, I remained unharmed, untouched by the storm's fury. With one final surge of energy, I managed to break the surface and fill my lungs with air.

"As the storm subsided and the waters calmed, I swam fiercely to the kayak that seemed miles away. I clung to the kayak, grateful for my survival. I felt immense relief that the brown leather satchel, securely fastened to the kayak's plastic bar, had not been lost in the tempest. I paused to catch my breath, my weary body *seeking respite.*

"The night sky continued its descent, the wind gently whispered its secrets, carrying with it a sense of anticipation. The once turbulent waves now seemed to offer gentle guidance, propelling me forward on my journey to the unknown. Exhaustion clung to me, a heavy burden on my weary shoulders. Yielding to its persistent call, I closed my eyes, surrendering myself to the gentle sway of the kayak and the lullaby of the water.

"Time passed, marked only by the rhythm of my breathing. My senses dulled, I floated between consciousness and dreams. The kayak carried me forward, its course dictated by unseen hands. As my eyelids fluttered open intermittently, I glimpsed the ever-changing landscape.

"Physically and emotionally drained, I offered my hand to the water, cupping it and drawing it to my lips. Fresh and invigorating, the taste awakened my senses, reminding me of the elemental force that surrounded me. Grateful for this sustenance, I continued to allow the kayak to chart its course. My grip on the paddle loosening as I surrendered to the unknown driven by an unyielding determination to discover what lay beyond the horizon."

Chapter 12

Caly Rose

"Reaching the other side of the lake, I looked back one last time admiring the pristine blue water. Not knowing where I was going, I sat on a nearby wooden bench, watching people watch me. It was fascinating, seeing them in their propeller machines that I later learned were cars. I saw how the car took them from one place to the next.

"'Ma'am are you okay?' a weary park ranger asked me as he apprehensively approached.

"'Excuse me, how do I get one of those machines?' I said, totally disregarding his question but happy to know I understood him and he understood me.

"'You mean a car? Ma'am, are you all right? Should I call an ambulance?' he said, looking concerned.

"The park ranger stood off to the side of me. His language was similar to what we spoke back home. The more he spoke, the more his words blended together. Still, it wasn't difficult to understand him. I was laser focused on obtaining a car. I knew my aching feet would not get me to the ley line energy I was being drawn to as it felt far away.

"While he stood there in mid-speech, still scanning over me, I rose up from the bench and proceeded toward the huge sign that read The Best Kept Secret on Turtle Island. North Manitou Island. The sign was fixed to a large building. Cars drove past and the people inside stared at me as I walked toward the row of buildings lining the street. One building grabbed my attention as I saw a man leaving out of the door holding what appeared to be food of some sort. Opening the door let out the savory smell of something being cooked. I followed the smell to the door of the place where the man came out of.

"I sure could eat. This food smells nothing like Marston though.

"Inside the building, I walked up to the counter, and sat down at the first empty seat I saw.

"A lady with curly black hair and dark brown skin walked toward me with a white food-stained apron on. Her face held a look of concern.

"'Ma'am are you okay? Usually customers wait to be seated but you look like you've been through it.'

"'I'm alive,' was all I could say in return.

"'Here's a glass of ice water. I'll put in an order for you, honey. It's on the house.'

"I nearly snatched the glass of cool water from her hand and quickly drank it down. She stood next to me until I finished and grabbed the empty cup off the table to refill it.

"'That cup was for you, this one is for the little one in there,' she said, filling the glass. I was overcome with embarrassment. The nice woman didn't seem to judge me before she walked to the back to get the food she promised me.

"Trying not to make eye contact with anyone inside, I kept my eyes plastered on the rectangle box that showed people talking and moving about. A woman appeared on the screen, her expression reflecting the gravity of a situation that recently unfolded in the forest. It was as if the surreal and the mundane were converging before my very eyes.

"The anchorman began, 'Ladies and gentlemen, we interrupt your regularly scheduled programming to bring you a breaking news update. Reports are pouring in about a cataclysmic event that took place right in the forest not too far from this town. Our reporters live near the site and are ready to tell us what they know.'

"The reporter immediately responded. 'Eyewitnesses are describing the scene as nothing short of extraordinary. An alien capsule crash-landed deep within the enchanted woods, defying all known laws of space and time. Government authorities are scrambling to secure the crash site and retrieve the remains of the capsule to investigate this unprecedented occurrence. Scientists, armed with curiosity and a thirst for knowledge, are venturing into uncharted territories, eager to decipher the secrets that lie dormant within the heart of the capsule. Authorities demand everyone avoid the area and report any suspicious activity or creatures. Speculation runs rampant around the town as to the intentions of these extraterrestrial beings and the mysteries they hold within their metallic capsule. Will this encounter reshape our understanding of the universe? Only time will tell. Back to you in the studio,' the reporter ended the segment.

"The weight of those words settled upon my shoulders, entwining me further into the tapestry of the moment. My crash landing had not only captivated the attention of this new world but had woven itself into the very fabric of my existence. It was a moment where reality and fantasy merged, where the unknown beckoned and destiny awaited.

"With an unspoken determination, I tore my eyes away from the rectangle box I later learned was a television screen. I knew my place was not among the passive observers yet, I was fascinated and fixated on it since those things didn't exist where I came from.

"The woman returned with my food and sat it in front of me. She pointed out everything on the plate.

"'Here's my famous chicken sandwich with lettuce, tomato, and pickle with a side of french fries. Would you like sauce with that?' Not knowing what sauce was, I nodded in agreement and proceeded to eat the sandwich

"All eyes were on me. The patrons watched me devour my food, eating everything on the plate and drinking the sauce from the small dipping cup. I was stuffed and well hydrated from the two glasses of water. Looking at my reflection in the mirror behind the counter, I no longer looked regal. My hair had been tossed about, royal garb ripped and stained with blood in some spots.

"Yes, I now understood the stares.

"'Is there somewhere I can go to clean myself up?' I asked the kind woman who had given me the free meal.

"'Of course, there is a restroom down the hall.'

"'I'm sorry, restroom? I don't understand.'

"'Come this way, I'll show you,' she said, ushering me toward her.

"What they called a restroom, we called a quick room because you get in there, do your business and leave quickly. There was no need to spend extra time there.

"Why would anyone want to rest there?

"I took a moment to check over myself in the mirror. Tears began to stream down my face. I missed my family and was thankful I was able to make it this far.

"When I returned from cleaning myself up, there were very few people left eating at the tables. I sat down in the chair resting my hands on the countertop to plot my next move. The woman was heading my way when the door opened and a man walked in taking her attention off me. As they continued to go back-and-forth, they barely acknowledged me leaving out of the front door. I walked over toward the car parked out front. I could see through the window of the building they were in full-fledged conversation not paying any attention to me opening his car door and getting inside.

"'Caly Rose what are you doing? You know nothing about cars,' I questioned myself.

"The car was on with the keys still inside. I grabbed hold of the circle wheel and began twisting it side to side hoping that it would somehow propel the car forward. But it didn't. My feet were plastered on the two-foot pedals near the floor of the car. I noticed pressing one of the foot pedals made the car screech a loud vroom noise which caught their attention inside of the building.

"The man bolted out of the door and began to yell and scream as he ran toward his car. I grabbed the long handle near the wheel as the man made his way toward the car. He grabbed hold of the handle on the car door. As he yanked the door open, the car jerked and took off down the road. I swerved in and out of traffic hitting several parked cars along the way until I got the hang of it.

"'Okay, Caly Rose, you got the hang of it. Keep going and don't look back.'

"It felt like hours went by driving down the road. I followed car after car heading in no particular direction, just wanting to get far away from the diner and the man whose car I had taken. The car started to jerk and putter along. I safely pulled over on the side of the road where I saw small children kicking a round ball back-and-forth in the grass. I got out of the car to stretch my legs since the baby began to kick against my rib cage. I found a nice spot on the green grass near the side of a large swimming pool that was away from the crowds but still in the view of my getaway *car. As I sat down, I couldn't help but reflect on how I had gotten here. Tears began to stream down my face thinking about my family back home.*

"'Calm down, Caly Rose. Breathe.'

"My mind grew quiet as my breathing slowed down. Focusing intently on the sound of the wind gently rustling the vibrant green leaves on the sprawling oak trees, I felt grounded. I felt connected. In total comfort, I let my mind wander to visions of the lush sprawling lands in Charcantium, of my beautiful family, and of my handsome husband RaKem.

"While sitting in the grass, I felt a strong jolt of energy travel through my body. I reached down with the palm of my hand spread wide and gently pressed deep into the grass. The energy traveled through my hand, up my arm, and throughout my body. As RaKem instructed me before I went through the portal, I trusted my instinct. I was where I needed to be.

"As I got up to head back to my getaway car, I saw a car with flashing red and blue lights parked right beside it. A man exited the car and started to walk toward my stolen car. Watching from a distance, he peered into the windows and opened the car door to take a look inside. I quickly headed toward the opposite side of the park to get far away from the scene.

"'It's going to be okay, Caly Rose. You'll find another car.'

"Walking down the road I still sensed the energy from the ley line and it grew stronger with each step I took in its direction. The dark sky signaled a storm was brewing. Sporadic raindrops turned to full on drizzle. The rain was cold, almost numbing to my aching body. I already knew what it felt like to go through the gates of hell. Rain was just the wind I needed to cool the fire.

"I reached down, grabbing the bottom of my stomach as the contractions started again.

"'Not right now, little one.'

"My baby was all I had in the strange place, and the emotions of me watching helplessly as the Bandrals kidnapped my children came over me. Leaning up against the brick building, the tears mixed with raindrops and stained my face. I moaned in pain, hunched over, cupping my contracting belly.

"Not too far in the distance, a group of men stood under the awning of a building, shielding themselves from the rain. As I continued to moan through

each contraction, one of the young men approached me. He was as tall as the corn stalks we grew in Chacantium.

"'Aye you good, Ma?' the young man proceeded to walk closer in my direction.

"I drew my makeshift weapon out from my sleeve and took a defensive position. My eyes began to glow and my breathing slowed. I concentrated on how I was going to kill him if he stepped any closer. Frozen in position with his hands in the air, the young man said, 'I was only trying to help your pregnant ass. You need to go to the hospital or something.'

"He slowly retreated back to the awning. The crowd he stood with watched him walk back in their direction. They laughed as he approached.

"'Haha, Ytwen just got dissed,' the other young man laughed loudly.

"'Man, shut up, Ellbey, she's just some pregnant homeless broad. She didn't want nothing anyway.'

"Holding my stomach, I continued slowly walking past the length of the dilapidated building. Car after car slowed down to notice me drenched in rain and physically in pain.

"One car slowed down and stopped. 'Ma'am, are you okay? My name is Bertha Jean. I'm a Licensed Nurse Practitioner and a Doula. You shouldn't be walking in the rain like this. You look like you are due any day now,' Bertha Jean said, looking concerned and talking to me through her car window.

"My weapon was still drawn in defense from my encounter with the young man. I was not interested in receiving help from this strange woman either.

"Parking her car against the curb, she reached in the backseat to grab something and exited the car. I drew my weapon as she got closer. She walked toward me with her hands in the air noticing my weapon.

"'I'm not here to hurt you. I want to help you. Let me help,' she insisted, inching closer and closer in my direction.

"I grimaced and grabbed my bulging stomach again, almost kneeling down to the ground from the pain of the contractions. A gush of water streamed down my leg. I looked at the woman in front of me.

"'Your water broke, didn't it?' she asked as if the look on my face was familiar to her.

"The fluid gathered in formation at the bottom of my feet. Bertha Jean and

I stood silent as we watched it circle around the bottom of my feet. The liquid continued to gather and swirl, not mixing with the rain falling from the sky. On cue, it glided over the side of the curb and down the sewer in front of the old rundown building.

"'We've got you out of this rain to deliver your baby,' she insisted, opening her umbrella to shield us from the rain.

"'Listen, I normally don't give rides to strangers but you are pregnant and I don't feel right just riding past you. At least let me take you to a hospital to deliver your baby then I will take you home.'

"'I can't go home. I don't have a home. I lost my family. My baby is all I got,' I said, fighting back tears until they started to stream down my face uncontrollably.

"'Hospital? I don't know what that is and I do not want to go there. No hospitals. Please just take me to your home. I can deliver my own baby,' I said adamantly.

"'My house it is. I'll help you deliver your baby. It's what I do for a living and I usually deliver at the hospital but since you insist, I will help you.'

"Hesitantly, I got in the car with the woman who was kind enough to check on me. Before we sped off into the rain, I got one last look at the area to remember where my water broke.

"'Where am I?' I asked Bertha Jean inquisitively.

"'You're in the state of Michigan,' she said suspiciously as if she could tell I wasn't from her town. 'Where are you from?' she asked.

"I ignored the question and continued to ride in the car silently until a contraction came with full force, making me moan in pain. I could tell she was in disbelief that a pregnant woman who could've given birth at any moment was out walking around the town at that time of the night.

"I looked out the window and tried to erase the images and drown out the screams of my babies being taken from me by the Parjeks. Life had never felt so empty. Looking out the window reminded me of how helpless I was at that moment. Anger rose within every fiber in my heart. I started to sob uncontrollably. Bertha Jean began to pat my back. I could see the tears well in her eyes, too.

"'My babies. I couldn't protect my babies. They're all gone,' I cried in anguish.

"'I don't know what happened to you, but whenever you're ready to talk about it, I'm here for you.' Betty Jean wiped away my tears. 'Honey, all this pain you're

feeling isn't good for the baby. Let's go inside to get you dried off so we can deliver your baby.'"

Chapter 13

Caly Rose

"That night, the relentless storm continued its assault outside, unleashing its fury upon the world. The thunder echoed through the house, its force shaking the very foundation as if an earthquake had been unleashed. Weariness enveloped me. My body drained from the arduous journey that brought me here. The imminent arrival of the baby left me feeling powerless, with no control over the unfolding events. Seeking solace, I found myself lying in Bertha Jean's guest bedroom, the storm's symphony of chaos serving as a backdrop to my thoughts. Closing my eyes, I focused on my breath, seeking a semblance of calm in the midst of the tempest.

"And then, like a guiding light in the darkness, RaKem's image flickered in my mind. His presence, even if only a memory, brought me a sense of peace and reassurance. I clung to that feeling, allowing it to anchor me in this uncertain moment.

"'It's time to push,' Bertha Jean's gentle voice broke through the storm's cacophony, drawing my attention back to the present.

"With each contraction, I summoned all the strength within me, pushing with unwavering determination. The very walls of the house quivered under the weight of the thunder's might, the elements outside echoing the intensity within.

"And then, amid the thunderous symphony, a cry pierced the air, announcing *the arrival of new life. Bertha Jean's skilled hands worked swiftly, guiding my baby into the world, clearing his airway with practiced ease. And in that moment, the storm's chaos seemed to fade into the background, replaced by the tender cry of my newborn son.*

"'It's a boy,' Bertha Jean affirmed, her voice filled with a sense of awe and wonder.

"She gently placed my crying baby on my chest, creating an intimate connection between mother and child. Gratitude washed over me, and my words spilled forth in a torrent of thanks and appreciation. Bertha Jean was a guardian angel, a source of safety and deliverance in this storm-tossed world. I held my baby boy close, cherishing the bond we shared, as she finished tending to the aftermath of birth.

"Tears of happiness streamed down my face, intermingling with the joy overflowing from my heart. This baby, this tiny being cradled in my arms, was more than just a child. He was a tangible link to RaKem, to Marston, to everything I held dear. His presence filled the void, offering solace and hope in a time of uncertainty.

"'What's his name?' Bertha Jean's curious question brought me back to the present, interrupting the cascade of emotions that threatened to overwhelm me.

"'His name is Michael. Michael Marston,' I responded, the name a testament to RaKem's desire had the baby been a boy.

"'Michael. That's a perfect name. Can I call him Mikey for short?' Bertha Jean's request carried with it a warmth and affection that mirrored my own feelings.

"'Of course you can. Thank you so much for all you have done. You saved my life, our lives. How could I ever repay you?' I asked, my voice filled with genuine gratitude.

"'No need for repayment, dear. This is what I do, day in and day out. I'm a doula, and it's my privilege to support and assist women in their journeys. You and Mikey are safe now. Rest and recover. I'll be just a staircase away if you need anything,' Bertha Jean's words were laced with a weariness that only highlighted her unwavering dedication.

"With a yawn that underscored her own exhaustion, Bertha Jean bid us good-night, retreating to find much-needed rest. Left alone with my baby boy, I gazed down at him, marveling at the miracle of life cradled in my arms. The storm

outside raged on, its echoes muted by the walls of the house. In this haven of peace, I allowed myself to succumb to weariness, my eyes heavy with sleep.

"As the night gave way to morning, I awakened to a sudden panic. Michael was no longer lying in the bassinet next to me that I'd borrowed from Bertha Jean. Alarm coursed through me, propelling me out of bed and toward the staircase, where snippets of conversation reached my ears. Bertha Jean's voice mingled with that of an unfamiliar woman, their words veiled in secrecy and unease.

"Creeping down the stairs, my footsteps silent, I positioned myself where I could observe without being seen. A Parjek woman stood before Bertha Jean, her presence a jarring reminder of the danger pursuing me.

"How had she crossed the portal? How had she tracked me here?

"Bertha Jean deftly handled the encounter, her words carefully chosen, masking the truth of our situation. She spoke of unwanted babies in need of temporary care, a narrative meant to deflect suspicion and safeguard our lives. The Parjek woman, seemingly satisfied with the explanation, inspected Michael from afar, her curious gaze lingering on him. Rage and protectiveness surged within me, my grip tightening on the staircase railing.

"Just as I prepared to take action, the Parjeks decided to depart, their true intentions veiled behind a facade of interest and concern. They bid their final remarks, their words laced with a mockery that sent shivers down my spine. Bertha Jean's suspicions were aroused, and she wasted no time securing the house, locking the doors with a determined finality.

"Moved by a mixture of relief and gratitude, I approached Bertha Jean, startling her with my sudden presence at her side. I expressed my deep gratitude for her unwavering support, for the protection she had provided to me and my newborn son. Her response was humble and heartfelt, assuring me that no repayment was necessary, that this was simply her calling as a doula. Her invitation to stay with her until I found my footing in the unfamiliar place filled me with a profound sense of awe and appreciation. It was an act of kindness that transcended the bounds of our short acquaintance, forging a connection rooted in compassion and understanding.

"'Bertha Jean, my name is Calynda Rose Marston, but you can call me Caly Rose. I come from a place called Charcantium, not too far from earth. Michael is the reason I'm here,' I confessed, allowing her a glimpse into the truth that lay at the heart of our extraordinary circumstances.

"'You're from another planet called Charcantium? Caly, my dear, are you feeling okay? You must be exhausted from this ordeal. It's okay. I'm not judging you. But you look pretty darn human to me,' Bertha Jean said sarcastically.

"'I know this may sound far-fetched but I am telling the truth and I will one day be able to show it,' I said reassuringly.

"'If this is so, Caly, you must understand sharing such information with others might lead them to misunderstand and misjudge you. It's essential to protect yourself and Michael. There are people who may perceive your story as a sign of mental health crisis and seek to intervene. But rest assured, I am here for both of you. You are not alone. Take the time you need, and when you're ready to talk, I'm all ears,' Bertha Jean offered, her words resonating with a mix of caution and genuine concern.

"Overwhelmed by the depth of her compassion, I allowed tears to flow freely down my cheeks. This woman, this stranger who had become my savior, was proof of the goodness which still existed throughout the universe. I thanked her again, my words inadequate to express the gratitude that swelled within me.

"'Caly, you can call me BJ,' she suggested, her voice filled with warmth and acceptance. 'When you're ready to share more, I'll be here to listen. But for now, I have a card game to host in a few hours. It's an exclusive club, Caly, with a select few members. You're more than welcome to stay downstairs and meet my friends.'

"Though I would have loved to stay and connect with the ways of earth, I graciously declined BJ's invitation and retreated upstairs to bond with my new baby boy.

"After putting Michael to sleep, I opened the bedroom door, and was met with a wave of fragrance that filled the hallway, thick and powerful. The scents of sweet fruits danced in the air, tickling the back of my throat and provoking a slight cough. As I descended the staircase, the scent grew even stronger, nearly overwhelming my senses. Yet, I pressed on, my eyes wide with anticipation.

"Reaching the bottom of the stairs, I found myself in the midst of a lively gathering. The music blared from the speakers, the rhythm pulsating through the room. Vella, one of BJ's friends, opened the door to a curvy woman who exuded *confidence and energy. The two of them shared laughter and inside jokes, their camaraderie evident in their easy banter.*

"Laughter and chatter filled the dining room as BJ's friends settled around the table, their voices rising above the music. I perched on the stairs, an observer of this boisterous scene, finding joy in their uninhibited expressions of friendship. Memories of my friends back home flooded my mind, and I couldn't help but smile at the thought of the adventures we would have shared.

"Unable to resist the lure of their infectious laughter, I quietly opened a drawer on the nearby side table, revealing a pad of paper and an ink pen. With a sense of purpose, I began to sketch out a plan—a plan that would lead me back to my husband, back to the world I had left behind.

"I quietly crept back upstairs to the guest bedroom where Michael was asleep peacefully in his bassinet. I resolved to pack away my worries, enclosing them in a metaphorical box hidden deep within my mind. Closing my eyes, I focused on finding inner peace, vowing not to let my fears consume me in this new place. The commotion downstairs seemed to fade into the background, replaced by a newfound determination to embrace the ways of earth. I was ready to immerse myself in this new world, leaving behind the storm-ridden past and embracing the present with open arms."

Chapter 14

Caly Rose

"**A**s the years passed, I integrated into the community and settled not far from the location where my water broke. The energy of that place still drew me in. It was important to me that Michael grew up in that area surrounded by children who looked like him. Our two-bedroom upstairs flat became our haven, a far cry from my home in Charcantium.

"Michael and I resided in the upstairs flat above Moonia and her parents. Moonia and Michael couldn't stand each other as children. They would constantly engage in water balloon fights or even throw eggs at each other. They had gained a reputation in the neighborhood as the bickering couple, a label they despised. I often reassured them that one day they would grow to like each other. That day finally arrived on the first day of high school when their tolerance for each other turned into something more—love.

"The neighborhood was my home away from home. I knew that the old rundown building, where my water broke, would be the perfect place to create Kaman Plaza. It was a challenge because it was condemned but I eagerly embraced it, knowing that Kaman Plaza would become a beacon of light for the community, and it was also the beacon of light I needed for RaKem to find me.

"Purchasing the condemned plaza for two hundred thousand dollars that I worked so hard for, I had a clear vision in mind. Despite many people not understanding why I wanted to buy the dilapidated building, I had a strong intuition guiding me. I wasn't just a believer; I was a knower. Trusting my instincts, I knew the area was the right place.

"During the construction phase, I would often drive past the site to monitor the progress when I wasn't traveling. I wanted everything to be flawless, leaving no room for imperfections when it came to Kaman Plaza.

"'We must stay on track, and everything has to be perfect for the grand opening,' I insisted during my meetings with the contractors.

"To show my appreciation, I would surprise the workers with catered lunches. The spread included Halal fried chicken seasoned with my special homemade house seasoning, a baked root vegetable salad with cubed beets, carrots, sweet potatoes, and turnips lightly drizzled with coconut oil, garlic and onion bush green beans, sweet homemade hot water cornbread, and fresh hibiscus tea sweetened with coconut sugar and freshly squeezed lime.

"'Mrs. Caly Rose, if you keep feeding us like this, we will fall behind on the project. If the food at your restaurants is as good as this, you can count on me to bring my family here every Sunday,' the stout project manager enthusiastically declared while indulging in each meal I offered.

"As the construction progressed, I traveled to various mineral and crystal gemstone miners around the world. These mines were located along ley lines, which produced some of the most magical, mysterious, and supernatural energy on earth. I was determined to partner with miners who ethically harvested crystals to sell in my store. I often stressed the importance of sourcing crystal gemstones and minerals carefully, avoiding any negative energy that might have been instilled by Mother Earth.

"'You have to be mindful of where you get your crystal gemstones and minerals from. You don't want to wear anything carrying bad karmic energy from Mother Earth. When people come to my store, they will find the best quality crystal gemstones and minerals that were ethically sourced,' I would often say.

"As the construction workers put the finishing touches on each storefront, the grand opening approached. The sight before me was exactly as I envisioned it. The entrance boasted a faceted copper gate and a quartz crystal–encrusted archway crown, shining so brightly people needed sunglasses to admire its beauty. In the center of the circular driveway, a massive copper water fountain adorned with a two-ton shungite stone took its place. The stone had not been up for sale, but I persisted until the miner agreed to sell it below his purchase price. On the left side of the plaza, a row of ample parking spaces lined the middle of the lot.

"I was involved in every aspect of Kaman Plaza and wouldn't have had it any other way. I conducted interviews, hand-picking each manager to run the stores. Over time, they became like family, Ytwen, Azrie, Vella, Essie, Mas, Nairam, and Sturdy as the store's managers. It was a unique establishment as it allowed community members to become members and actively participate. To become a member, individuals paid a monthly fee, and membership was only offered once a year or when a spot became available. Members gathered quarterly to discuss community economics, decide which foods to carry or discontinue, and determine how to distribute profits or reinvest them back into the business. Gatherers' welcomed anyone to shop there, although membership was exclusive to the local area.

"On the night of the grand opening, Moonia stayed behind to help me close up the store as a thunderstorm brewed outside.

"'Moonia, you didn't have to stay. I could've managed on my own. I truly appreciate all your help,' I said, walking over to hug Moonia and gently rubbing her bulging belly. 'Any day now, little one,' I insisted.

"'Moonia, before we go, let me perform a healing session on you as a token of my gratitude for all your assistance. You and my son have been my source of strength throughout the years.'

"'Momma Caly Rose, you know I can't resist. I would love that. Besides, I've been experiencing some aches and pains lately. Thank you for doing this.'

"I proceeded to perform pranic natural healing energy techniques on Moonia as she lay on the chakra healing bed. She rested comfortably on her side, her head resting on a silk pillow with a copper hue.

"Moonia, Michael, nor the rest of the world had any idea of our extraterrestrial origins, nor of the portal I had been preparing. But in that moment, as I focused on healing Moonia, my mind couldn't help but wander to the portal, to the possibility of finally seeing RaKem again, reuniting our family.

"'Momma Caly Rose, you seem distracted. Is everything alright?' she asked, breaking my train of thought.

"I paused for a moment, taking in her concern. 'Moonia, there is something I need to tell you and Michael. It's a secret I've kept for everyone's safety. Let me go next door to fetch him. Stay here and rest. I want to share this with both of you together,' I said, my tone serious.

"'Alright, Momma Caly Rose. The baby seems to know something exciting is happening,' Moonia said, a touch of sarcasm in her voice. 'Ouch, something's happening!'

"My heart skipped a beat as I noticed a small spot on the floor, evidence that Moonia's water had broken. The baby was coming, regardless of the revelations I had in store. I quickly locked the door and closed the blinds, shutting out the raging storm outside.

"I hurried next door to find Michael, knowing time was of the essence. When we returned, Moonia's contractions had intensified, signaling that the baby's arrival was imminent.

"'Michael!' Moonia called out, her voice filled with urgency.

"He reassured her, 'We will deliver the baby here.'

"Gathering towels and blankets from the supply closet, I prepared the makeshift delivery room. As I glanced over at Moonia, lying on the bed, a realization struck me. I had become so wrapped up in thoughts of the portal and reuniting with RaKem that I had almost forgotten about the imminent arrival of the baby.

"But there was no time to dwell on my own desires. Moonia's labor progressed rapidly, her pain intensifying with each contraction. The storm outside mirrored the tension in the room, adding an air of urgency and anticipation.

"I caught sight of the spot on the floor where Moonia's water had broken. It seemed to come to life, the fluid swirling and dancing around her in a mesmerizing display. Memories flooded back to me—the night my own water broke, the water guiding me to the copper singing bowl. And now, in this extraordinary moment, history was repeating itself.

"Moonia's water, seemingly animated, gathered in a pool beneath their feet and directed her and Michael toward the copper singing bowl at the center of the room. Confusion and fear filled their eyes, and I could understand their apprehension. But deep down, I knew that this was part of a larger plan, part of the opening of the portal to Marston.

"The water doubled, then tripled, then managed to multiply until it expanded enough to suspend Moonia and Michael in the air above the singing bowl.

"The blue water, defying gravity, slowly lowered them to the bottom of the singing bowl, settling them inside, an ethereal scene unfolding before us.

"'What's happening, Momma?' Michael cried out. 'Enough with the tricks!'

"Excitement welled up within me. Moonia and Michael had no idea what was about to happen, no inkling of the portal that was opening before them. But as the blue water settled in the bowl, my focus shifted to the miracle of birth, to the baby who would soon join us on this extraordinary journey. The anticipation of reuniting with RaKem would have to wait, as the present moment demanded my attention—the arrival of new life, the beauty of the unknown, and the magic that lay before us.

"Moonia and Michael tried to maintain a calm demeanor, though confusion and apprehension filled the air. This was the moment I had been waiting for, the moment I needed to share my revelations with them. The swirling blue water ceased its movement. The hanging quartz crystal trembled, emitting a vibrant and luminous beam of white light that pierced through the center of the water and the bowl—an unmistakable sign of the portal's activation.

"'The portal!' I exclaimed with jubilation. 'Moonia and Michael, you two are the key to the portal.'

"Moonia's eyes widened, and she glanced at Michael, seeking understanding. 'Portal? What portal? Ahh! Michael, the baby! We can't go through a portal while I'm in labor! Momma Caly Rose, what is happening?'

"'Baby, I don't fully comprehend what's happening, but we must deliver our child. Momma Caly Rose seems to have some understanding. Let's trust her,' Michael assured Moonia, his voice filled with reassurance and determination.

"Meanwhile, the water descended, revealing a hidden staircase beneath the copper singing bowl.

"As Moonia and Michael descended the staircase, I followed closely behind, my heart fluttering with nervous anticipation. The unknown lay before us, and everything was unfolding rapidly. It was time to reveal the truth of their identities, to shed light on the secrets I kept hidden for far too long.

"At the bottom of the staircase, we were confronted by three magnificent gold doors, each adorned with intricate locks, gears, knobs, and pulley systems. Michael couldn't help but voice his curiosity. 'Momma, were these doors always here?' he questioned.

"'Michael, I witnessed the construction of this place from its inception. This isn't of earthly origin; it's a gift from our home. But now, we must focus on the imminent birth of your baby,' I replied, urging them to prioritize the task at hand.

"The water beckoned us toward the middle doors, leading us into what I now dub the River Room. As if granting permission, it gently released Moonia and Michael from its watery grasp, collecting in the center of the empty rectangular pool. In a mesmerizing display, the water multiplied in size, swiftly filling the space from end to end. And as we ventured deeper, the room seemed to stir from its slumber, awakening to our presence.

"With each step, the glossy obsidian–black floors beneath our feet came alive, shimmering and pulsating with an otherworldly energy. Assisting Michael in finding Moonia a seat, her cries of apprehension grew louder. In response, the water transformed, shape–shifting into a staircase that beckoned us to bring Moonia closer.

"'Wait a minute. I'm not getting in there,' Moonia protested, her voice laced with fear and tears streaming down her cheeks. 'Can't you two call an ambulance? This is insane.'

"Yet, the water shifted, gliding down to where we sat, and caressed the side of Moonia's cheek with gentle reassurance. It seemed to have a calming effect, imbuing her with a sense of peace and trust. Michael, standing nearby, remained skeptical, his posture defensive.

"'Momma, it's time to start talking,' Michael demanded, his voice laced with frustration. 'What do you know? What have you been hiding from me? You expect us to trust you and this...this big puddle of water?'

"I took a deep breath, feeling the weight of the secret I carried for so long. 'Michael, I have kept a great secret from you, one that could endanger us all. But today, the portal has opened, and now it's time to reveal who you truly are. We must trust the process.'

"'Trust the process?' Michael scoffed, his eyes filled with a mixture of confusion and anger. 'I don't even know who you are anymore, Momma. My wife is about to give birth any second now. You want us to follow the guidance of this water that could drown us? Enough is enough. We're leaving. Come on, Moonia.'

"But before they could take a step, Moonia cried out in anguish, clutching her stomach. 'Ahhh, Michael, the baby! She's coming!' Her voice trembled with pain. 'Michael, I don't understand all of this, but I trust your mother. She would never put us in harm's way. Look around, Michael. Fate has led us here. Don't you want to know what's next? Let's get this over with.'

"Moved by Moonia's strength, Michael and I exchanged a glance, his face a mixture of apprehension and admiration. We stood by Moonia's side, facing the water staircase. And as if in unison, we locked hands, our feet stepping onto the watery steps.

"One by one, we ascended the staircase, our bodies partially immersed in the water as it swirled around us. Slowly, it whisked us around in a circle, forming a whirlpool that separated us from one another. Without warning, the water collapsed, engulfing us in its depths, silencing our screams as it severed our connection.

"Emerging from the depths, we bobbed to the surface like buoyant vessels. Together, we swam toward the pristine white sand bank that awaited us. Michael immediately tended to Moonia, ensuring her safety after the disorienting ordeal. As I looked around, a sense of familiarity washed over me, finding solace in the breathtaking beauty of the expansive cave.

"The vibrant blue water shimmered as it gently crashed against the white sand, mirroring the colors of the sky. Above us, the ceiling was adorned with swirled marble in hues of purple, green, and blue, from which emerald icicles dripped, casting an otherworldly glow. The damp cave walls were illuminated by the soft luminescence of blue-green glowworms, lending an ethereal ambiance to our surroundings.

"It became clear that we were no longer beneath Kaman Plaza in the River Room. We had entered the sacred cave of Mt. Summit on the planet Charcantium, a place where my ancestors had once connected with divine energy through the vibrations generated by the emerald cave.

"Moonia's voice broke the hushed air, her words a whisper. 'Where are we?'

"'This is my home,' I replied, a sense of purpose emanating from within. 'We are on the planet Charcantium. I need to find RaKem.' My urgency surged as I started to make my way toward the cave's exit, momentarily forgetting Moonia's impending labor.

"But the water rushed forward, blocking my path, as if knowing my desperate attempt to save RaKem was not part of the plan. I pushed against it, my heart sinking with each futile effort.

"'What are you doing?' I questioned the water, my voice filled with both pleading and frustration. 'This is my only chance to save my husband. Please, let me pass.'

"But the water stood its ground, unyielding. It had a purpose, one I couldn't fathom at that moment. My body sank to my knees, surrendering to the inevitable, as tears welled in my eyes, mingling with the damp cave floor.

"'Momma,' Michael's voice called out, drawing near as he tapped my shoulder. 'Listen, my wife is about to give birth. A cave is not the ideal place we had in mind. We need answers, Momma. What are you hiding?'

"The anger in Michael's voice stung, piercing through my heart. There was no escape from this conversation, no way to evade the truth any longer. I owed it to them, to Michael and Moonia, to reveal who I was and how their existence was intricately woven into the fabric of this night.

"'Momma,' Michael persisted, interrupting my thoughts, his voice filled with urgency and anger. 'You haven't acknowledged a word I just said.'

"'Michael, I owe you both an explanation,' I began, my voice tinged with a mixture of weariness and determination. 'But first, let's tend to Moonia. The birth of your daughter is imminent, and she deserves a safe place to enter this world.'

"Turning slowly to look at him, I couldn't help but notice a shiny object that protruded from the glowworm-laden cave wall just behind him. It seemed to invite me, a sparkling mystery that held secrets yet to be uncovered.

"I could tell Michael's mind raced with newfound information. The idea of being an alien, of belonging to another world, left him reeling. He glanced around, his gaze falling upon a shiny object protruding from the cave wall. Curiosity got the better of him, and he carefully extracted the object—a rectangular box, meticulously crafted with lines of petrified wood and quartz crystal in various hues.

"'It can't be. But it is! The Tetratetum!' I exclaimed in astonishment, recognizing the familiar symbol engraved on the front. The box refused to yield, its intricate lock system resisting our attempts to open it.

"'The Tetratetum will only reveal its contents to the chosen one—the descendant of the Jewel's lineage, who embodies mind, body, soul, and spirit. It's a box of immense power and significance, with secrets hidden within,' I recited, reading the inscription on the box's underside.

"My focus shifted from the Tetratetum to Michael as he assisted Moonia. Carefully placing the box beside them, I guided Michael on how we would deliver the baby.

"The cool blue water crept closer to us on the sandy beach, inching with each movement we made. It enveloped us, gently caressing our skin as we moved backward against the cave wall, partially submerged. Moonia's contractions grew stronger, signaling the imminent arrival of the baby. The water sparkled, its surface shimmering as it swirled around us, guiding us away from the wall and toward the center of the cave.

"'Wait a minute! I am not getting back into that water to deliver my baby!' Moonia hollered.

"With a graceful dance, the water wrapped around Moonia's body, lifting her into the air against her will. She helplessly ascended toward the top of the cave, where a small opening allowed the moon's radiant light to shine upon her. I swam alongside Michael, watching in awe as Moonia hung suspended in the air, supported by the water's gentle embrace. And then, in a moment of magic, the baby emerged from the depths of the water, into Moonia's waiting arms.

"Tears of joy streamed down Moonia's face as she cradled her newborn daughter. The water swirled downward, adorning Moonia in a flowing purple Charcantium gown, complete with a golden and quartz crystal tiara. Michael glanced down at himself, noticing the transformation that had taken place. The water had adorned him, his mother, and the baby in traditional Charcantium royalty attire, signifying their lineage.

"Curiosity and wonder filled the air as I leaned in, eager to catch a glimpse of my beautiful granddaughter. 'What is my granddaughter's name?' I asked softly, my arms reaching out to hold the precious bundle.

"'Na'Ray wanted to name her baby sister Shaylah. She even got Dash on board with the name. Shaylah Marston she is,' Moonia replied, her voice filled with tenderness as she admired her daughter.

"I cradled Shaylah gently against my body, feeling a surge of pride and love. Walking through the water toward the center of the cave, I could feel its gentle current guiding me. It swirled around me, a protective cocoon as I held my granddaughter close.

"'I, Caly Rose Marston, wife of the great RaKem Marston, stand before you, my honorable and benevolent ancestors of love and light, with Shaylah Marston, the heir to the Darkest Light,' I spoke proudly, my voice echoing through the cave. Michael and Moonia watched on, still puzzled by the events unfolding around them. It was time to reveal the truth.

"Approaching Moonia, I gently placed the sleeping Shaylah back into her arms. Michael and Moonia looked at me expectantly, their eyes filled with questions. They deserved answers, and I was determined to provide them.

"'Michael Marston, you are the son of the Darkest Light here on the planet of Charcantium,' I began, my voice filled with a mixture of solemnity and anticipation. 'Today is a day of great significance, except... I had expected your father, RaKem, to be here when the portal opened. The year I arrived on earth, your father and the Beholder came to Mt. Marston to reveal the next Darkest Light. But that day, tragedy struck. The Parjeks, visiting from Parjeka, killed your father's best friend Michael, his trusted Beholder and kidnapped your brother, sister, and many other Jewels and Beholders. I know nothing of their fate and have longed for them for many, many years. Before entering the portal, your father told me he saw you and your wife sleeping, with a beautiful baby girl at the foot of your bed. I was certain when Na'Ray was born she was the Darkest Light, but nothing happened on the night she was born. Today, however, everything has aligned, except RaKem is not here,' I explained, my voice tinged with sorrow.

"'Momma, don't you think this is something you should have told me? I'm an alien, that's all I keep hearing. A royal alien. You should have allowed me to choose my own fate. Moonia deserved to know, too,' Michael's voice carried a mixture of anger and frustration.

"Moonia interjected, standing between us, cradling Shaylah protectively. 'Things happen for a reason. We are here for a reason. Regardless of who and what you are, *nothing will change the love I have for you and our family. If I had to do it all over again, I would choose you every time,' she said, her voice filled with unwavering support and love.*

"*Feeling remorse, I reached out to hug Moonia, seeking forgiveness. But the water suddenly thrashed against the cave wall, violently drawing our attention away. It projected images of armed Parjeks marching toward the cave, their intentions clear. The urgency to leave the cave and find RaKem welled up within me, but the sheer number of Parjeks outside the cave made it an impossible task.*

"*Acting swiftly, I grabbed a handful of dirt from the cave floor and placed it in a pouch I noticed beside me. Moonia held Shaylah tightly, and Michael embraced them, drawing them close as we climbed back into the water portal. The water guided the Tetratetum into my hands, its power pulsating through my veins. With a sense of urgency, we were transported back to the River Room beneath Kaman Plaza, the rushing water carrying us swiftly through the portal and into safety.*

"*The room welcomed us, its tranquil aura providing a brief respite from the impending danger outside. We caught our breath, taking in the sights and sounds of the familiar space. The air felt charged with anticipation, as if the room itself knew the weight of the revelations that had unfolded.*

"*Moonia cradled Shaylah in her arms, her eyes fixed upon her daughter. Michael stood by her side, a mix of worry and determination etched on his face. I knew they sought more answers, understanding, and a sense of purpose amid the chaos that had enveloped our lives.*

"'*Michael, Moonia, there is much I must share with you,' I began, my voice steady and filled with determination. 'But let us first find refuge and safety. We must regroup and gather our strength to face the challenges that lie ahead.'*

"*Moonia nodded, her eyes reflecting both trust and uncertainty. Michael's gaze held a flicker of determination, a willingness to confront the unknown. We stood together, united in our purpose, as the River Room surrounded us with its watery embrace.*

"*In that special sacred space, we would uncover the truths, unravel the mysteries, and forge a path toward a future that held both peril and promise. And with Shaylah, the heir to the Darkest Light, cradled in our arms, we were certain to navigate the shadows and emerge victorious in the face of adversity.*

"As we returned to the River Room, the water calmly spread across the pool, and I directed my attention to Shaylah, who had been peacefully resting nestled in her father's arms. I asked Michael to hold her as I took her in my arms, gazing into her innocent eyes. 'Shaylah, my precious granddaughter, this day, the day of your birth, is one of the most significant in my life,' I whispered softly.

"The water glided toward Moonia, gently placing a necklace upon Shaylah's swaddled form—a necklace adorned with a rare Marston gemstone. 'Shaylah, you are a beautiful and special baby girl. I will ensure you are prepared to embrace your birthright as the Darkest Light. You see, Moonia and Michael, Shaylah is the chosen one. She carries the weight of destiny upon her tiny little shoulders,' I explained, a mixture of pride and concern in my voice.

"Moonia and Michael, still grappling with the revelations and the gravity of the situation, exchanged glances, their love and determination evident. 'Shaylah, my love, we will always stand by your side. We will protect and support you, no matter the challenges that lie ahead,' Moonia declared, her voice filled with unwavering motherly support and devotion."

The blast from the past ended and the water screen receded back into the pool. I looked over to Moonia first, who was nearly half asleep, and then at Shaylah, who looked curious. Her hand rested on her cheek as she watched the visual memory the water provided like a cinematic movie.

"Wow, Grandma Caly Rose, that was deep. It was beautiful and tragic. I'm sorry you have been holding this secret from me for so long. It must be hard being here without your husband. But, I am a child. How do you expect me to save my grandfather and your planet? Your surprises have been life-altering. I'm afraid to discover what lies next," Shaylah expressed, weariness seeping into her voice as she approached the water's edge.

"And, if Grandpa RaKem possesses such magical powers, why can't he use them to defeat the Parjeks and live happily ever after?" Shaylah's words dripped with skepticism and disbelief, revealing the doubts and uncertainties that plagued her young mind.

"Moonia, bring Shaylah by my house tomorrow. There is something I must show her, something that will shed light on her questions and guide us on the remainder of our path," I urged, understanding the weight of her doubts but knowing that the time for action had come.

"I'm so looking forward to what else is in store," Shaylah sarcastically conceded.

"Momma, we'll swing by the store tomorrow after Shaylah gets out of school. I promised my coworker that I would introduce her to you. She's bringing her daughter along. And yes, Shaylah, you're coming, too," Moonia interjected, shifting the conversation to a more mundane topic, though the mysteries of the portal and the Tetratetum still loomed over our heads.

"But, Momma..." Shaylah began, her protest cut short by Moonia's firm resolve.

"No 'buts,' Shaylah. You heard what I said. Fate has brought us to this moment, and we will face it together, as a family," Moonia declared, her voice leaving no room for argument.

"Alright, ladies, don't be late. There is much for me to teach you, Shaylah. Be prepared for whatever may come our way. Earth is no longer safe, and those who seek to harm you are relentless. Your mother and father can no longer shield you from the dangers that await. You have to stay ready. Do you understand? The Parjeks could be anywhere and in alliances with anyone. Even students at school," I cautioned, my voice filled with determination and concern as they made their way to Moonia's truck.

As they walked out of the building, I couldn't help but feel a mix of emotions—hope, apprehension, and a deep longing to see RaKem again. I knew our journey had just begun, and there were many trials to face, secrets to uncover, and battles to fight. The road ahead would be treacherous, but with family by our side and the powers that awaited Shaylah's activation, we would persevere and fulfill our destinies.

Chapter 15

Geni

The next morning, Momma excused me from school. I settled onto the living room couch, the image of Shaylah's impenetrable pouch replaying in my mind. It remained stubbornly closed, defying all efforts to reveal its secrets.

All the planning, all the anticipation, had led to this moment—for Shaylah I bet. I wonder what was inside.

"Geni, pay attention," my mother's voice snapped me out of my reverie. She stood near the dining room wall with a cup of steaming hot tea. her actions deliberate and purposeful. I watched, curious and intrigued by her mysterious behavior.

"Uh, Mom, what are you doing?" I asked, my curiosity getting the better of me. This was an entirely new side of her I had never witnessed before.

"Shhhh," she hushed me, her gaze piercing. She commanded my silence with a single look, and I straightened my posture, captivated by the unfolding scene.

Without warning, the wall shifted and morphed, forming a pattern of dancing blue and red squares until they settled into the shape of a door. My mother stepped through the door and retrieved a black rectangular box, her movements confident and purposeful.

"Geni, come here. The box will only open when it scans you," she beckoned me, her voice filled with an air of intrigue.

I approached the box, its sleek black surface intriguing me. An orange laser scanned my face, turning a deep shade of purple, and a copper lever was released. With a decisive pull, my mother opened the box, revealing a dazzling copper dagger nestled inside. It was a thing of beauty, unlike anything I had ever seen. The handle, encrusted with black tourmaline, fit perfectly in my hand. Engraved on the shining metal blade were the words "Dagger of Death."

"Once you have Shaylah cornered, you know what to do. We only have one chance to eliminate her. This is it, Geni. We cannot afford any mistakes," my mother declared, her tone firm and resolute.

"I understand," I replied reluctantly, a sense of unease washing over me. "But do we really have to do this to her, Mom? I mean, that girl may not be who you think she is."

"Listen, Geni. Don't bag out on this. If we don't eliminate her, she will learn to harness the powers of the Charcantium Crystal. And we cannot allow that to happen," my mother explained, her voice tinged with urgency and determination.

"Okay, Mom," I acquiesced, my doubts temporarily pushed aside as I focused on the task at hand.

The rest of the day, I researched Shaylah's entire family, learning more about them and Charcantium. The sound of a horn interrupted my research session, signaling it was time to leave. Shaylah and her mother were waiting outside, parked in the driveway. My mother gave me a final pep talk before we stepped out the door. With a press of a button, my dagger compressed and disappeared into my purse. As we approached the car, I couldn't help but notice Shaylah's gaze fixed upon me from the back seat.

"Hey, girl. This is my daughter, Geni," my mother introduced me to Shaylah's mother, Moonia.

"Hi, Geni. I'm Moonia, and this is my daughter, Shaylah. Oh, my, you are very pretty. I love your purse, too," Moonia complimented, her words filled with genuine admiration.

"Well, you know what Grandma Caly Rose always says— 'They dress poison in pretty little packages all the time,'" Shaylah interjected, her tone laced with sarcasm.

"Thank you for the compliment. Yes, Shaylah and I go to school together," I replied, my voice icy as I reached for my bag, hoping Shaylah's mother wouldn't recognize me as the girl who bumped into her in the hallway at Brookhaven. It didn't matter to me if she remembered; after all, her family did unspeakable things to my father—they deserved more than a mere bump.

To no surprise, Shaylah didn't bother to respond, and her mother glanced at me through the rearview mirror a few times, suspicion evident in her eyes. Each time, I subtly motioned my head in a different direction. Moonia and my mother engaged in conversation about work and their desire for changes in the office, but Moonia's forced smile betrayed her discomfort whenever her gaze shifted in my direction.

We arrived at Kaman Plaza, the sight even more awe-inspiring up close. I sought reassurance from my mother, but she remained focused on the mission, not even sparing me a glance. Shaylah looked my way, and I mustered enough composure to say, "Is there something on my face?" My tone dripped with annoyance.

"Yeah, your face," Shaylah retorted cruelly.

At that moment, any remnants of hesitation I had about eliminating her vanished. I was starting to feel justified in my decision. Perhaps this was the universe's way of delivering justice for my family. My resolve hardened, and I couldn't wait to fulfill my mission.

Momma and I stood together by the car, preparing for the task at hand. She reminded me to maintain a clear mind, cautioning against any signals that could tip off Shaylah. We trailed behind Shaylah and her mother as they approached the door, but we paused momentarily, pretending to admire the vibrant flowers adorning the building's entrance.

"Momma Caly Rose isn't with a patient," Moonia remarked, continuing toward the door. "The flowers are truly magnificent, aren't they? Take your time to appreciate the surroundings and sheer beauty of this place before we go inside."

Shaylah, in her usual sardonic manner, chimed in, "Yeah, my grandma grows mushrooms in her garden, too," casting a sarcastic glance in my direction before continuing toward the building.

My mother sensed the brewing tension and amusement danced across her features as Shaylah mentioned the mushrooms.

"Geni must have told you how much we love mushrooms. We spend hours scouring the farms to pick them," my mother quipped.

Shaylah retorted, her wit' sharp as ever, "Yeah, those 'moron' mushrooms, right?"

I couldn't help but snap back, correcting her with a touch of irritation and cold stare, "They're called Morel. And for the record, I'm looking at the real 'moron' here."

Moonia swiftly stepped in, placing herself between us to divert the escalating exchange. "Ladies, let's keep the peace," she interjected, attempting to defuse the tension.

"Moonia's right, ladies. We're here to get to know one another. I can sense that you two must be the best of friends at school," my mother chimed in, injecting a touch of lightheartedness into the situation.

Tuh. She wishes.

My anger surged within me. This was the moment, the opportunity to rid ourselves of this irksome waste of everyone's time. My focus sharpened, my determination unyielding. There was no turning back now. With a subtle nod from my mother, the signal was clear—it was time to act.

My mother and I positioned ourselves on either side of Shaylah, making our way down the path. I discreetly secured the Dagger of Death, ensuring its easy accessibility for the strike. Shaylah stared straight ahead, seemingly oblivious to my actions. I swung my fist toward her side, intending to strike her, but she swiftly caught my hand before it could make contact. Undeterred, I swung with my other hand, only to have it deftly caught as well. She was fast.

In the blink of an eye, my mother lunged toward Moonia, swiftly overpowering her and sending her crashing to the ground. Meanwhile, Shaylah headbutted me forcefully in the forehead, almost knocking me off balance. As I stumbled, I witnessed Shaylah rushing to help her mother, and an elderly woman with gray locks hurriedly ushering them inside the store. The door closed, nearly hitting me in the face.

Determined, I reached for the door handle, twisting it with all my might. The knob glowed a searing orange, scorching my palm and fingers. I grimaced, clutching my injured hand, while Momma unleashed a barrage of kicks on the door, each strike causing the bolts to loosen, the door gradually giving way under the assault. Suddenly, a blinding beam of light pierced through the room, crashing down upon the building. It cascaded along the walls, sliding from the roof to the ground with a dazzling radiance. While Momma continued her relentless assault on the door, a surge of electricity coursed through her body, propelling her backward and sending her crashing to the ground.

My heart raced as I rushed to her aid, seeing the extent of her injuries from the fall.

"Come on, Geni, we must go now. Shaylah used her powers and has already activated a protective barrier surrounding the building. We will return and eliminate her before she fully harnesses her powers," Momma spoke with icy determination, her anger directed toward the store's entrance.

Momma and I departed, leaving Kaman Plaza behind. I cast a backward glance, noticing Moonia observing our departure from the store's window. The pain in my hand transformed into seething anger as thoughts of killing Shaylah consumed my mind.

The journey back home remained silent, with Momma and me taking turns checking for any signs of pursuit. The only accompaniment to our walk was the foreboding presence of dark clouds swarming the evening sky.

"How did she know?" Momma seethed with anger as we stepped through the doorway of our house. "I've done everything in my power to keep Moonia oblivious to my true nature in that wretched job."

"Momma," I hesitated, reluctant to share the truth. "I didn't mention that I accidentally bumped into Moonia in the hallway yesterday when she visited the school."

"What do you mean 'bumped,' Geni?"

"I mean I physically collided with her, nearly knocking her off her feet."

"Really, Geni? How could you keep such a significant incident from me?"

"I'm sorry, Momma. I didn't think it was necessary to divulge."

"Necessary? You didn't think it was necessary to inform me? Our entire mission is now jeopardized. They know who we are. Tonight, we must eliminate them, or else..."

"Or else what, Mom? You've kept me in the dark for far too long about this mission. All I know is that you trained me to recognize the symbol on Shaylah's pouch, and I am the one tasked with ridding the world of her. But why me, Mom? Why?"

"Because you are part Beholder, that's why. You are the legacy. By eliminating Shaylah, all the Jewels' powers will transfer to you, and our family will rule the Charcantium. That is why."

"Part Beholder? What is a Beholder?"

"I can only share what I've been entrusted to know. Your father informed me that his lineage hails from a long line of Beholders originating from a planet called Charcantium. It is an Earthlike planet, but one that was once inhabited by extraordinary beings capable of remarkable feats. Your father would regale me with stories for hours on end about the enchanted Charcantium crystals, superhuman abilities, and force fields. Initially, I thought he was simply weaving tales to fill our nights, but I was mistaken.

"One day, your father and I were approached by a young woman and a man who claimed to be Parjeks from the planet Parjeka. They sought our assistance in avenging your grandfather, Michael's, death. They divulged that Shaylah's grandfather, RaKem, murdered your grandfather and that Shaylah's grandmother resided here on earth. They informed us that Shaylah's grandmother had given birth to a son named Michael, and they had been tracking her ever since she'd given birth to him here. They knew precisely where to find Michael and his family. Your father joined forces with one of the Parjeks to surveil the Marston family, plotting to capture Michael and his entire family, dead or alive. Preferably dead. Before your father left, he told me that if he didn't return, I should assume he was dead. This occurred fifteen years ago, the night Shaylah was born," Momma recounted.

Suddenly, everything fell into place. "So, that's it. Momma, you could have simply told me. I would have kept this secret," I spoke sharply, my tone laced with frustration.

"Revealing the symbol was sufficient. Besides, I wanted you to experience as much normalcy as possible, despite the fact that you are anything but normal."

"But Momma, they never found Daddy's body, right?" I inquired, seeking some semblance of closure.

"Those individuals are ruthless. They would never allow us the dignity of a proper burial for your father. Instead, we honor him in our own way," Momma's voice filled with sadness as she generously applied a homemade salve to my injured hand.

Silently, I absorbed the weight of Momma's revelations. She wrapped my hand with a white cloth bandage infused with aloe and healing herbs, preventing the blister from spreading. Thoughts of the justice our family deserved echoed in my mind. The very justice I was determined to deliver upon Shaylah and her family. I understood my purpose more clearly than ever. Nothing could stand in my way. Sipping my tea, I watched as Momma activated the surveillance system and arranged an arsenal of weapons on the living room table. While we were safe within our home for the moment, Momma prepared for an all-out war, summoning Barbara and Maxwell, Parjek allies for reinforcements.

Chapter 16

Shaylah

"**S**haylah, if you can hear me, Geni is the girl that went out of her way to aggressively bump into me at your school the other day. Don't react. Just keep looking straight ahead and continue walking forward. Be prepared for anything, I don't trust her," Momma telepathically urged.

"Yes, Momma. She hates me. And she wasn't at school today but she doesn't look sick to me," I replied telepathically, understanding the gravity of the situation. I could sense the relief in her voice that I had heard and followed her instructions.

As we neared the door of Grandma Caly Rose's store, Geni swung toward me, but I swiftly caught her fist inches from my face. She attempted another swing, but once again, I intercepted it. I noticed Momma lunging in our direction, but Geneva grabbed her and slammed her to the ground. A fiery rage surged through me, and I headbutted Geni with all my might, knocking her off balance. I rushed to help Momma to her feet, and in that moment, Grandma Caly Rose swiftly ushered us into the store.

"Hurry, Shaylah. Stand inside the copper singing bowl," Grandma Caly Rose instructed, her voice filled with urgency.

I quickly moved to stand inside the bowl, while Momma locked the door with a huge, glowing, hot-iron lock. The tension in the room heightened as

Momma took up a defensive position, warning me that Geni had the Dagger of Death in one hand and was reaching for the door with the other.

Geni attempted to open the door but badly burned her hand from the scorching hot-iron. Geneva directed her to the side and angrily started kicking the door with great force. The bolts rattled and loosened with each kick. Grandma Caly Rose hurried to the door, observing Geneva's futile attempts.

"Wow, she's one pretty lady with evil and vengeance in her heart," Grandma Caly Rose remarked.

"Momma Caly Rose, as you always say, they dress poison in pretty packages all the time. And evidently, their children, too. I had to be reminded of that," Momma responded, her gaze focused on me, anxiously standing inside the copper bowl.

"Moonia, they are amateurs. I see the girl has the Dagger of Death, but she doesn't even know what to do with it. I'm sure she's been instructed to kill Shaylah and get the Tetratetum," Grandma Caly Rose explained.

"Kill Shaylah? Over my dead body. They won't get a chance to touch a hair on my baby's head," Momma declared fiercely.

"What they don't know is that we have more than just the Tetratetum. RaKem sent me here with the Book of Jewels. It's our first line of defense in places outside of Charcantium. It's an ancient spell book that will allow the Darkest Light to activate the protection spells inside with just one Marston crystal before gaining all of the powers inside the Tetratetum. I have kept it hidden here all this time. The Tetratetum and the Book of Jewels are never to be kept in the same place. That's why I asked you and Michael to take the Tetratetum and keep it safe," Grandma Caly Rose revealed.

"About the Tetratetum," Momma interjected.

Concern etched across Momma's face as Grandma Caly Rose abruptly walked away, cutting off Momma's sentence. She approached a cabinet and opened a secret compartment, revealing a weathered leather book with a metal clasp. Handing me the elusive book, Grandma Caly Rose's actions caused the Charcantium crystal on my bracelet to glow.

I felt a mix of apprehension and excitement. Everything was happening so fast yet in slow motion. My breathing grew heavy, but Grandma Caly Rose sensed my distress as I stood inside the copper singing bowl.

"Shaylah, the sacred spells in this book will only activate when the Darkest Light has a Charcantium crystal in hand. Your bracelet has one of the stones. I need you to repeat after me. But in doing so, say it confidently. Say it loudly. And most importantly, say it with dominion," Grandma Caly Rose instructed.

"With dominion?" I questioned.

"Yes, baby, with dominion. As if you are the Darkest Light and have the true power to rule over the spells in this book and activate them," Grandma Caly Rose reassured me.

She began to speak, and I repeated after her, my voice resonating with confidence and authority.

"I, Shaylah Marston, granddaughter of the great RaKem Marston invoke my divine birthright protections as the heir to the Jewel Throne. I, Shaylah Marston, ask that you protect all that I see as my sacred sanctuary and let no harm come to me as I prepare to assume the powers of the Darkest Light, the one true guardian of the Charcantium crystals and commander of the rogue roots."

Geni and Geneva were still kicking away at the door when Momma yelled out, "Hurry, the door won't hold much longer! What's taking so long?"

Grandma Caly Rose didn't understand why the protection spell didn't activate and I didn't either. I recited everything with dominion just like Grandma told me to. I closed the spell book and ran my fingers around the embossed edges. There was a small latch I unhinged and pricked my finger. I almost dropped the book. The hinged retracted back inside with a drop of my blood, causing a small wooden tablet to pop out from the side. I gently wiped the dust from it, exposing engraved words.

"Earth bend and water flow, I conjure the rogue roots as I go. Light as the air and heavy as the sea, bestow your powers unto me," I recited out loud and with dominion.

The huge quartz crystal suspended in the air directly reflected the light from the sun concentrating it in the center. A stream of blinding white light began to swirl above me, wrapping around my body. Momma and Grandma Caly Rose proudly looked on in amazement. Right before their eyes, I turned from a solid human being into a hologram. Suddenly, a wave surged from the gemstone bracelet on my wrist. It glowed bright purple, illuminating my hand. I extended my hand outward to engulf the entire room in the bright purple hue.

"She's doing it, Moonia!" Grandma Caly Rose hollered out in excitement.

The entire store began to vibrate. Waves of protective light energy shot out through the roof of the building, creating a protective barrier.

As Geneva attempted one last kick, the barrier sent her flying back, falling hard on her backside. Thick reddish-brown roots shot up from the ground and encased the entire building, leaving a small opening for us to see outside of the store.

"They're leaving, Shaylah. Whatever you're doing, don't stop. They are almost near the gate and the roots are covering the entire building," Momma encouraged.

I'm getting better and better at this.

With a newfound sense of confidence and power, I kept the protective energy flowing, closing my eyes to focus. All was silent within my thoughts. No worry, no doubt could be found. My soul rested gently within my body. This time, I had nothing to fear.

"I'm so proud of you, Shaylah," Grandma Caly Rose said as she approached me. "You are the Darkest Light and who you are destined to be. Now that they know who you are, I know they will come back. But this time, they will need an army. Moonia, bring Shaylah and the Tetratetum to the card game tonight."

Momma interjected, "Momma Caly Rose, about the Tetratetum, we asked our friends to keep it safe for us."

"You did what?" Grandma Caly Rose responded, her tone filled with surprise and concern.

"We didn't want you to worry that night Shaylah was born. We were attacked that night by two men. Michael killed one of the men, and the other... Well, we found out his name was Jackson. He's been held at our friend's house in a secure bunker."

"He's being held at the same friend's house where the Tetratetum is?"

Grandma Caly Rose questioned.

"Well, sort of. Kind of. Well, yes. But I can assure you, the Tetratetum is safe. Jackson has been held there for over fourteen years now in the holding cell underneath their basement. There is no way for him to escape."

"I can't believe you two kept this from me," Grandma Caly Rose expressed her surprise.

"Momma Caly Rose, Michael and I agreed that telling you that night would have caused unnecessary worry. We woke up the next morning to find Shaylah's crib encased in thick reddish-brown roots. The one's inside of her crib were burned. We thought Shaylah was injured due to a large bloodstain on her sleeping gown. We didn't know what to do. We're sorry for keeping this from you, but we trust our friends completely. Besides you and the elders, they are the only people we trust," Momma explained.

"Time out, Momma. What friends?" Grandma Caly Rose interrupted, feeling left out and confused.

"Saqq's parents have the Tetratetum and the prisoner," Momma revealed.

"So Saqq's parents know who we are?" Grandma Caly Rose asked, my curiosity piqued.

"Yes, Momma Caly Rose, Saqq's entire family knows about us. That's why he's always looking out for Shaylah when we aren't around," Momma confirmed.

"I feel like I'm the last person to know anything around here. Are you really my momma, and are you really my grandma?" I couldn't help but interject in a smug tone.

"Hey, watch it young lady. Your parents and I have done our best to give you as normal of a life as possible, knowing that one day we would have to tell you everything—the family secrets, your true identity. We didn't know how it would all play out. I hope you understand how difficult this is for all of us, Shaylah," Grandma Caly Rose explained, her tone firm but understanding.

"Sorry, Grandma Caly Rose. It feels like my life is changing every hour. Now I've got to save the world," I lamented, regretting my smugness.

"You are the gift we have been waiting for, Shaylah. You are protected by legions of ancestors, angels, and gods who will not let any harm befall you,"

Grandma Caly Rose reassured me. "We have work to do, good work. And no more secrets from each other. I'm locking up the store and grabbing some supplies. I'll meet you at my house."

Momma and I got into her SUV and headed to Grandma Caly Rose's house. She kept talking on the speakerphone to Daddy, Na'Ray, and Dash, explaining the events at the store with Geni and Geneva.

Minutes later, we arrived at Grandma Caly Rose's house. Aunt BJ was already there, opening the door to let everyone inside. Earth, Wind, and Fire's "Fantasy" played softly on the radio, and the scent of burning white sage filled the air as we entered.

As I made my way to the dining room, I stopped in my tracks, dropping the bags I was carrying. My mouth hung open, and my eyes widened in confusion and surprise.

"What the—" I couldn't find the words to complete my sentence.

"What the what?" Grandma Caly Rose asked, her tone daring me to finish.

Everyone was there—Uncle Jensiah, Aunt Vella, Uncle Ytwen, Uncle Azrie, Aunt Essie, Uncle Mas, and Aunt Nairam. But they weren't my real Great-Aunts and Uncles. They were members of the community and most importantly, Grandma Caly Roses' friends. She insisted they were to be addressed as Aunt or Uncle so and so. But they were all gathered here, their spiritual selves floating above their physical bodies, engaged in a card game.

Grandma Caly Rose placed her hand on my shoulder. "What do you see, Shaylah?" she asked, curious about my reaction.

"Well, Grandma Caly Rose, I see everyone, but I see two of them," I said, stunned.

A chain of blue crystals linked together formed a thin barrier at the arched entryway to the dining room. It constantly shifted, changing appearance every two seconds. I blinked, trying to merge the flickering figures floating above each person's head with their physical bodies.

"Shaylah, Aunt BJ has been taught a cloaking protection spell. She casts it every week over the elders during our card games," Grandma Caly Rose explained.

I looked up at the ceiling, searching for clarity, but found nothing. Their higher selves remained suspended above their soul star chakra, meditating while their lower selves peered into the playing cards.

Unfazed by the music and commotion, Aunt Essie descended from her higher self and approached me. "Shaylah, we have been waiting for you," she said, her voice filled with warmth. The others looked in my direction, smiling.

"You see, Shaylah, you are not alone. We have elders here on earth who will fight alongside you to help us. They are of pure heart and help to safeguard our family secrets. We call it the card game because we play the cards we are dealt and accept all outcomes. Your presence here tonight is one of them."

Momma walked through the barrier and, with the crystal necklace she put on, she too could see the elders floating above their physical selves. I realized that the necklace was the same one Grandma Caly Rose had made for Aunt BJ. It allowed them to see the spiritual realm.

Uncle Ytwen descended from his higher self, tall and slender, with dark skin and long locs cascading over his shoulders. He gathered seven crystal bowls and arranged them in a half circle, returning to his higher self, adorned in traditional royal garments, his hair neatly braided.

Momma sat at the other end of the table, and Grandma Caly Rose fetched another chair from the closet. It sat at the head of the table.

"Here, Shaylah. This seat is for you," Grandma Caly Rose said, guiding me toward it gently.

"Grandma Caly Rose, did Daddy make this chair?" I asked, admiring its beauty.

"Yes, spirit guided your father when he created this magnificent chair for you," Grandma Caly Rose expressed with gratitude.

My name was carved into the wood at the top, and carnelian, jade, and lapis lazuli crystals adorned the armrests. Two quartz crystal globes were perfectly positioned for my hands. The feet of the chair were embellished with diamond points. I sat down, a wide smile spreading across my face as I settled into the cushioned seat.

Uncle Ytwen took a rubber mallet and began to rhythmically strike each crystal bowl, producing a beautiful humming sound. Aunt Nairam joined in, chanting in a melodious voice. Her higher self emitted a radiant white light from her hands, her eyes beaming with the same luminosity. The light cascaded across the room, converging on me.

Grandma Caly Rose led the chant, her voice resonating with power. "I, Calynda Rose Marston, wife of the great RaKem Marston, am here with my granddaughter, Shaylah Marston, the heir to the throne of the Darkest Light. We call upon the Almighty Universe to grant Shaylah Marston safe passage through all realms and bless her as she claims her birthright powers by safely opening all portals to past, present, and fifth dimensions."

A subtle vibration began to rise from the legs of the chair, gradually intensifying. I looked down, observing my lower self fully engrossed in the card game. I noticed that my hands were clad in purple tight fitting forearm length gloves, and I wore the same dress as before, the one I had worn when I first discovered my powers. I was fully dressed in Charcantium garb, complete with a crystal crown made of solid gold and quartz crystal. The vibration continued to surge, and I closed my eyes, allowing myself to be enveloped by its energy. All became silent.

When I opened my eyes, I found myself suspended above the earth, seated among the brightest stars in the universe. My higher self had detached from my physical form, and I felt a sense of freedom as I explored the universe around me. But Grandma Caly Rose's voice reached me, urging me to return.

"Shaylah, tonight is the night we return to the store to open the portal. Only you have the power to do it," she called out. "You must return now, you can explore the universe after we've secured the Charcantium crystals and the Tetratetum."

"Yes ma'am. I'm ready. I can do this," I responded with determination.

She handed me a small gold rectangular box with my name engraved on it. With anticipation, I opened it and discovered a pair of earrings and a beautiful crystal-encrusted gold ring.

Grandma Caly Rose carefully placed a set of intricately crafted earrings in my ear. Each one gleamed with ancient symbols, pulsating with dormant power. "These were specially designed and handmade just for you, Shaylah," she explained, her voice carrying a sense of reverence. "They are to be given to you on this day as you continue your journey to becoming the Darkest Light."

I marveled at the craftsmanship of the earrings in the mirror, feeling a surge of anticipation and responsibility. They were not mere accessories, but vessels of untapped potential, waiting for me to unlock their secrets. I slipped them onto my wrists, the cool metal sending a shiver of energy up my arms.

As the others gathered their gear and packed their cars, a sense of purpose filled the air. Momma's voice floated through the phone, relaying the events to Daddy and keeping him updated on our progress. We set out once again, returning to Kaman Plaza, where Daddy awaited us. It was time to regroup, to prepare for whatever lay ahead, from our charged encounter with Geneva and Geni.

Chapter 17

Shaylah

D addy had patiently awaited our arrival, parked by the gate of Kaman Plaza. The sprawling reddish-brown roots had entwined the entire plaza, creating an impenetrable barrier. The entire community was out in full force viewing the spectacle from behind the caution tape. Grandma Caly Rose signaled Daddy to follow behind her car to the entry on the backside of the building that had not yet been taped off by the heavy police presence.

We all hurriedly exited the vehicles to approach the door covered in roots. As I approached, a sliver of an opening emerged, just wide enough for me to pass through, as though I held the key to its unlocking. Hastily, I guided everyone inside, and as we crossed the threshold, the protective dome of roots sealed shut behind us. Walking through this organic fortress felt both awe-inspiring and humbling, as if we were being embraced by the very essence of nature itself. The same reddish-brown roots that shielded us also wrapped around the entrance of the Ground Source Healing Center. Acting on instinct, I approached the door, and to my amazement, the roots gracefully parted, granting us entry.

Daddy switched on the television, and the screen flickered to life with a breaking news alert from the local police, urging residents in the surrounding neighborhoods to evacuate immediately. The warning spoke of armed and dangerous individuals who had seized control of the area. Images of me, Momma, Daddy, and Grandma Caly Rose flashed across the screen, accompanied by claims that we were armed and dangerous, and should surrender peacefully. The distant whir of helicopters resonated in the air as we sought refuge within the confines of Kaman Plaza.

I commanded the roots to create a small opening by the window, allowing us a glimpse of the outside world. Army tanks lined the streets, their imposing presence accentuated by the menacing weaponry they bore. In defiance of evacuation orders, a group of protestors stood behind yellow caution tape, brandishing signs in support of our family. The chaotic scene outside, coupled with the smear campaign unfolding on television, demanded our immediate attention as we focused on the task at hand—the opening of the portal. Daddy and Momma stood side by side, anxiously awaiting Na'Ray's call.

"Listen carefully, this is not a drill. It's the real deal. Find Dash and make your way to the nearest empty room with a television. Keep your phone in your pocket and don't use it until you're together," Daddy's voice resonated with urgency as he instructed Na'Ray.

Observing Daddy pacing back-and-forth only heightened our unease as we awaited Na'Ray and Dash's call. The wait felt interminable, but finally, Daddy's phone rang three minutes later, piercing the tension in the air. The relief in Daddy's voice was palpable as he spoke briefly, his words carrying love and reassurance.

"So glad you two are safe. Turn on the television. Do you see what they're saying? This is happening right now, as we speak, and time is running out. We love you both very much. You can do this. This is just like we've practiced, okay? Mutetartet, Mutetartet, Mutetartet," Daddy's words lingered in the air, imbued with a profound sense of faith and determination.

"What does 'Mutetartet' mean?" I couldn't help but ask, curiosity piqued.

"Mutetartet is Tetratetum spelled backward. It's the name of the box we entrusted to Saqq's parents, the one containing the key to amplifying your powers. But using it incorrectly can have dire consequences that span generations," Daddy explained.

"Daddy, if they are labeling us as armed and dangerous, aren't they in extreme danger? We have to do something," I said, my concern evident for Dash and Na'Ray.

"Shaylah, relax. Na'Ray and Dash are capable of taking care of themselves. They've been trained for this day. We trust them, and they'll join us soon," Daddy assured, attempting to assuage my worries.

As time pressed on, the anticipation grew. The vibrations of the copper bowl I stood within intensified, and the quartz crystal embedded in it emanated a radiant glow. The portal began to open, compelling us into action. Daddy, Uncle Mas, and Uncle Ytwen remained upstairs, ready to defend our position, while the rest of us hurried down the staircase. Guided by Grandma Caly Rose, we made our way to the third door—the doorway that would transport us to Marston, our final destination.

"Shaylah, using a circular motion with your hands, open the first lock," Grandma Caly Rose instructed, her voice imbued with both wisdom and anticipation.

The entire building trembled as the lock disengaged, causing the door to come alive, untethering itself from the wall. I stood beside Grandma Caly Rose, my eyes closed, attuning myself to the energies swirling around me.

"Be prepared, everyone. They are here. I can sense Geni," I announced, the weight of the impending danger palpable in my voice.

Daddy's urgent voice echoed from the portal, compelling us to hasten our efforts. "They're about to send missiles! Open that portal now!"

As the second lock released, the door swung wide open, unleashing a torrent of dust and energy into the room. We watched in awe as a shadowy figure emerged from the other side—the very figure we had been expecting. Her long, neatly braided cornrows cascaded past her collarbone, her skin as smooth and rich as melted chocolate, reminiscent of Daddy's.

Startled, she gazed at us, mirroring our own astonishment. However, none were as stunned as Grandma Caly Rose, whose expression seemed to convey that she had just seen a ghost. The beautiful woman stepped forward, out of the portal.

"This can't be," Grandma Caly Rose uttered, her voice trembling with a mix of disbelief and joy.

"Momma?" the young woman exclaimed, rushing into Grandma Caly Rose's open arms.

"You're really alive," she whispered, tears streaming down their cheeks as they embraced.

"Vania, I thought they had taken your life. I saw them... I saw them take you all away..." Grandma Caly Rose's voice wavered, unable to complete her sentence.

"Momma, the Parjeks couldn't extinguish our light. We were part of their plan all along. They showed you only what they wanted you to see. They wanted you to believe we were dead," Vania explained, her voice laced with determination.

"Wait, so you mean to tell me that Denise and Ellbey are alive, too?" Grandma Caly Rose's voice quivered with a mix of hope and astonishment.

"Yes Momma, we are all alive and well. I was meditating earlier, connecting with my higher self when a powerful electromagnetic pulse led me to a secret portal in the woods. It was the same portal Daddy used to tell me stories about when I was a little girl. And it brought me here," Vania shared, her eyes gleaming with memories.

"Oh my goodness, Vania. You remembered!" Grandma Caly Rose's voice quivered with a mix of awe and gratitude.

"How could I forget, Momma? You and Daddy told the most incredible stories," Vania replied, a soft smile gracing her lips.

"Where are Denise and Ellbey?"

"Denise just married the next in line to the Parjeka throne, and Ellbey is married to the Princess of Parjeka. They are arranging their marriage to solidify the bloodlines," Vania explained, her voice tinged with both concern and determination.

Just then, Grandma Caly Rose turned her attention to me, taking my hand gently and guiding me toward Vania. "Vania, this young lady is your niece, Shaylah. She is the one who emitted the electromagnetic pulse that brought you here. She is the reason I know RaKem is still alive. But now, it's time for us to save him. For her to save Charcantium from the Parjeks."

Vania glanced at me, her eyes filled with a mix of surprise and admiration.

She gracefully stepped forward, bowing her head slightly. The gesture caught me off guard, but I sensed the honor in her presence.

"It is a great honor to meet you, Shaylah. Wow, I have a niece. That means..." Vania's words trailed off, a realization dawning on her.

"Yes, I gave birth to your brother Michael a few days after arriving on earth. He's upstairs, holding down the fort. This is his wife, Moonia," Grandma Caly Rose introduced, swiftly acquainting us all.

As Daddy, Uncle Ytwen, and Uncle Mas hurried down the stairs, panic etched across their faces. Daddy explained four planes armed with bombs were set to destroy Kaman Plaza and everything within a mile radius. The countdown had already begun, giving us less than an hour to gather everyone and enter the portal. Grandma Caly Rose remained undeterred, her focus fixed on introducing Aunt Vania to Daddy.

"Alright, alright, Michael, we can discuss doomsday later. Right now, I want you to meet someone," Grandma Caly Rose insisted, leading Daddy toward Aunt Vania.

"Hello, Michael. I'm your sister, Vania. You bear a striking resemblance to our father," Aunt Vania greeted Daddy, her voice filled with a mix of nostalgia and warmth.

"Wait a minute, who are you? Vania? How did you get down here?" Daddy's head snapped toward Grandma Caly Rose, disbelief etched across his face.

"Yes, Michael. This is your sister, Vania. She accessed the portal because Shaylah activated an electromagnetic pulse that Vania harnessed during her meditation," Grandma Caly Rose clarified, her voice carrying a note of conviction.

Daddy took a step back, studying Vania intently. I could see the admiration and recognition flicker in his eyes as he observed their shared chocolate-toned skin and familiar features. Momma, on the other hand, seemed troubled, her thoughts entangled in a web of emotions.

Daddy stood back, his eyes fixated on Vania. The resemblance between the both of them with rich chocolate skin, was undeniable. Momma, on the other hand, wore a troubled expression, lines of worry etched across her face.

"Michael, it's been at least twenty-five minutes since we said Mutetartet to

Na'Ray and Dash," Momma voiced her concern, her tone filled with anxiety.

"They know they must retrieve the Tetratetum by any means necessary, but it shouldn't take this long. Saqq's home is not too far from their school and Na'Ray is a good driver. They should've been here by now," Daddy said while consulting with Momma in a nearby corner of the room on a backup plan he devised. The way Momma looked, I could tell she wasn't happy about what Daddy came up with but the embrace he gave her seemed to provide a sense of calm as they both approached me.

"Shaylah, as much as I don't like this idea, you are the Darkest Light, powerful enough to handle your own. We are going to need you to leave to find your sister and brother and retrieve the Tetratetum. You're the only one small enough to fit through the drainpipe that leads to the Royal Park's swimming pool. From there you will be able to make your way to Dash and Na'Ray. But you have to hurry, Shay. The longer you're away from Kaman Plaza, the weaker the rogue roots become, leaving this entire site vulnerable to attack."

Grandma Caly Rose cleared a path, revealing the drainpipe that awaited my descent. Enclosed spaces weren't my comfort zone, but I had to summon inner strength to push through. Equipped with a backpack prepared by Grandma Caly Rose, I was ready. Just as Daddy was about to close the drain door with me inside, Grandma Caly Rose intervened, prompting him to wait.

"Shaylah, everything you need is in that bag," Grandma Caly Rose emphasized. "When you reach the drain at Royal Park's swimming pool, twist all four corners of the hatch door backward, then pull the lever upward. Twist the handle out, and push into the grooves. This will catapult you into the deep end of the pool by the diving board. Be cautious; they're open for night swimming."

Dash and Na'Ray occupied my thoughts as I maneuvered my way through a labyrinth of underground tunnels. Above ground, chaos ensued. As I ascended the ladder of the storm drain for a closer look, a woman's voice washed over me, overwhelmed by emotion.

"Joe, they're going to blow up Kaman Plaza and anyone inside in forty minutes for not complying with law enforcement orders. We better get away from this place," the unknown woman cautiously expressed to the man.

Forty-five minutes left. Time is slipping away. I better hurry.

Finally, I reached the pool's drain opening. The four metal corners turned backward effortlessly, allowing me to pull up the lever. With a bit more force, I twisted the handle out and pushed into the grooves, unleashing a rush of water that propelled me into the diving section of the pool, just as I was warned by Grandma Caly Rose.

I propelled myself forward, slicing through the water's surface, swimming the length of the pool until I reached the shallow end with its inviting steps. The lifeguard's whistle pierced the air, drawing attention to my fully clothed state. Thinking quickly on my feet, I concocted an excuse. "I just got so excited I had to jump in," I offered, flashing a smile as I hurried toward the girl's locker room.

Inside the locker room, I opened the flattened backpack, discovering Grandma Caly Rose hadn't exaggerated. It contained everything I needed, including dry clothes and shoes, which I swiftly changed into. A small groove in the wooden panel of the building revealed a hiding spot for my wet attire. I quickly shoved them inside.

As I exited the locker room, a familiar face, stood before me. Concern etched across Tray's features as we exchanged words.

"Shay, I knew it was you," Tray's voice carried a mix of surprise and concern. "What are you doing here?"

Glancing around cautiously, my voice was laced with urgency as I replied, "Tray, I've heard the rumors circulating in the neighborhood and in the news. Fifteen minutes have slipped away, and I still haven't reached Saqq's house. My entire family is at Kaman Plaza, and they're in grave danger. I don't have time to explain but it's really bad and I have to hurry."

The weight of the situation hung heavy in the air as we stood together, our hearts pounding with a shared sense of urgency.

Tray's eyes reflected her understanding. "My mom and dad are waiting for me outside. Let me try to talk to them. Shay, you need their help. Walking to Saqq's house from here takes about twenty minutes. You wouldn't make it back in time."

With a determined nod, Tray hurried off, leaving me alone in the bathroom stall to seek assistance from her parents. The voices of other girls echoed in the locker room, discussing my family and their predicament. To my surprise, an adult locker room attendant shut down the gossip, expressing hope for me and my family's safety. It was a small act of kindness amid the swirling rumors that engulfed the small town.

A few minutes ticked by, and eventually, Tray returned, her expression revealing a hard-fought battle with her parents, which she had emerged victorious from.

In Tray's parents' car, I observed Tray's dad, his eyes periodically flicking toward me. His emotions were palpable, and I could sense his unease about my presence.

"What have you and your family done that they want you dead or alive?" Tray's dad asked, a mixture of concern and caution in his voice. "You know what, the less I know, the safer we'll all be. Just keep me in the dark, and my family won't be in danger."

Reluctantly, Tray's dad dropped us off a short distance from Saqq's house. He insisted that Tray not accompany me, but Tray's determination prevailed. As the car pulled away, we proceeded cautiously down the alley toward Saqq's house. Every noise we encountered made us take up defensive stances, casting furtive glances over our shoulders.

With a dagger in hand, I stealthily approached Saqq's backyard alongside Tray. Surprisingly, the dogs remained silent, failing to alert Saqq's family to our presence. They looked fearful with their tails tucked and let out small whimpers.

I ascended the stairs to the patio door, noticing it was already slightly ajar. Peering inside, I discovered the kitchen in disarray, completely torn upside-down, evidence of a thorough search.

Without warning, a brilliant blue flash of light illuminated the room, accompanied by a spine-chilling scream that pierced the air. Tray and I cautiously stepped into the kitchen, only to be confronted by two figures clad in sleek black tactical gear. It was clear they hadn't come for peaceful negotiations. In a defensive stance, they positioned themselves side by side, brandishing long rods with rotating, expanding fireballs of reddish-orange hue at the ready.

Observing the lethal weapons before us, I couldn't help but comment to Tray, "Why is it that the villains always seem to possess the most formidable arsenal?"

A voice, dripping with malice, resonated from beyond the kitchen, drawing our attention away. "Well, well, well, if it isn't the Darkest Light herself," the voice taunted. "Step right in, Shaylah. Everyone's been waiting for you, except your big-mouthed sister, who's currently tied up at the moment. You must have heard her scream. Guess you won't have to deal with her anymore. I despise older siblings. That's why I eliminated all of mine!" The voice laughed maniacally as it continued to spew hateful words, fueling the already tense atmosphere as Tray and I were coerced to move toward the living room.

As we entered, a distressing scene unfolded before us. Saqq, Dash, and Saqq's parents were bound to chairs, their bodies marred with bruises and smeared with blood. Dash sat motionless, bleeding profusely from his nose and mouth. Rushing to his side, I gently wiped his face, trying to offer some comfort amid the chaos. However, my actions were swiftly interrupted when the two imposing figures seized me by the wrists, forcibly dragging me to the forefront of the room. Desperately scanning the space, I searched for Na'Ray, but she was nowhere to be found.

"So, you're the troublemaker who's disrupted my quality time with my new wife," the burly man declared, his voice dripping with venom. "I despise that I have to kill you and then go back to kiss your aunt, who is now my wife. You should've perished the day you were born, but your father eliminated my brother before he could finish the job. Thanks to my niece, Geni, sniffing you out, I have the opportunity to kill you, your siblings, your friends and to right this wrong that your family has done."

Just as the hulking man uttered the final words of his sinister speech, I contorted my wrist with a swift movement, deftly slipping free from the tight grip of the Parjek soldiers. Their fiery scepters lashed out in response, the scorching tips grazing the side of my face, leaving a trail of searing pain. Instinctively, I clutched the burned flesh in my hand, a mix of anguish and fury coursing through me. A blaze of rage ignited within me as I embraced my newfound power. Drawing my gleaming dagger, I fiercely engaged in combat, expertly warding off the two assailants that encircled me. With each punch and kick, my strength surged, and miraculously, the gash on my face began to heal.

A radiant, fiery white glow emanated from my dagger, casting an ethereal light upon the chaos unfolding. Swiftly dropping to one knee, I skillfully wielded my dagger to sever the thorny bindings constricting Dash's wrists. In a serendipitous moment, Dash inadvertently brushed against the handle of my dagger, and the wounds on his body miraculously closed, his vitality restored. Emboldened, he swiftly joined the fray, fearlessly confronting the Parjek soldier wielding the scorching scepter.

Tray found herself in the back corner of the room, locked in a fierce battle with a tall, slender Parjek woman. Sensing the urgency, Dash gestured for me to assist Tray. With a swift and precise strike, I incapacitated the Parjek woman, rendering her unconscious by striking her with the obsidian obelisk statue. At the same time, Dash skillfully disarmed the other Parjek, forcefully knocking the scepter from his grip. The man's desperate cry echoed through the room, "Kill the girl in the basement!"

Without hesitation, Dash thrust the scepter deep into the man's chest, causing him to crumple to the floor. Urging Tray and Saqq to aid his injured parents, Dash and I wasted no time in rushing downstairs to the basement, where a chilling scene awaited us.

"Ah, Shaylah Marston, what a predicament," the man sneered, his knife pressed menacingly against Na'Ray's throat. He reveled in his sadistic display, yanking her hair back to reveal her bloodied, swollen face. "Your sister certainly put up a fight, didn't she?" he remarked, nudging the lifeless leg of his fallen comrade aside.

He maintained a tight grip on the knife, shifting his body to the other side of Na'Ray while slowly dragging it across her neck, revealing trickles of blood.

"Kneel down slowly and slide your dagger toward my foot. Make a single wrong move, and I'll end her life before yours," the man remarked.

I cautiously descended to the ground, my heart pounding with apprehension.

However, Na'Ray's subtle wink provided a glimmer of hope. I carefully maneuvered the dagger toward Na'Ray's foot, but just as it neared her, she stomped on the rim of the blade, propelling it into the man's neck. Blood spurted from the wound as he collapsed to the floor. Swiftly, I severed the thorned cords that bound Na'Ray's wrists, placing the dagger in her trembling hand, and together, we raced back upstairs.

In the living room, Saqq, Tray, and Saqq's mother surrounded Saqq's gravely injured father. I attempted to place the dagger in his hand, hoping its healing magic would revive him. However, the dagger's powers were only effective on those of Jewel descent.

At that moment, Saqq's mother approached her curio cabinet and skillfully manipulated a hidden lever, revealing a secret compartment. From within, she retrieved a weathered brown leather satchel and a first aid kit. She gently placed the satchel in my lap and attended to her husband's wounds.

"Open it," she commanded, her voice laden with urgency while preparing his bandages.

Eagerly, I unfastened the satchel and withdrew the Tetratetum. The petrified wood box, adorned with shimmering quartz crystals, gleamed in my hands and emitted a faint scent of aged timber. The locks on its front seemed to come alive, swirling in a mesmerizing dance as I cradled it on my lap. However, opening the box without the guidance of Grandma Caly Rose was not an option.

"We need to bring this to my grandmother," I declared, rising to my feet. But before I could make my escape, Saqq's mother approached me with a sense of purpose.

"Shaylah, there's something you need to see," she said, taking my hand and guiding Dash and me toward the basement stairs. I handed the Tetratetum to Na'Ray and followed Saqq's mother down into the dimly lit basement. As we reached the second platform of the staircase, we halted before a wall. Saqq's mother tapped the top of a large family photograph, and to our surprise, the wall trembled and vibrated, revealing a concealed handle. She turned the knob, unveiling a secret chamber within the basement. Stepping into the dark chamber, I noticed a double-sided mirror that allowed us to observe the other side. There, on the mirrored wall, the two Parjeks we had left to bleed out were visible, their life forces drained away.

In the far corner of the room, a man sat, chained to the wall. Saqq's mother approached him cautiously, and he slowly rose from his crouched position.

"Shaylah Marston. The day you were born, I tried to kill you," the man said. "Today is the day you have stepped into your powers I see and these people are keeping their word by releasing me?"

His words hung heavy in the air, suffused with the weight of past transgressions and present desperation. The man's voice held a mixture of bitterness and resignation, his admission an unsettling revelation. Around us, the atmosphere crackled with tension, each breath charged with anticipation.

"Not so fast, Jackson. I knew this day would come. Where you would see the light of day. The day that I would ask you for help. You are a Beholder, please heal my husband and you are free to go," Saqq's mom pleaded, her voice trembling with a blend of fear and hope, imploring for a miracle. Her words were laden with the raw vulnerability of a wife pleading for the life of her husband. The room seemed to hold its breath, as if time itself paused to bear witness to the unfolding moment.

"Heal your husband? He's the one who shot and captured me. Now you want me to heal him?" the man said sarcastically.

The imprisoned man stood there, a complex tapestry of emotions etched across his face. Confusion, remorse, and a flicker of reluctant compassion danced in his eyes. He grudgingly considered the plea before him, grappling with the conflicting forces that tugged at his conscience.

"We could've killed you a long time ago. I even kept up with your daughters' milestones and brought you pictures of her regularly. I've been more than a good host to someone who tried to kill my best friends and their children," Saqq's mom insisted.

The air crackled with a charged energy, as if the very fabric of fate hung in the balance. In that moment, the room became a battleground of emotions, a collision of past grievances and the possibility of redemption.

He seemed to weigh the choices before him. Rubbing the grooves that were left behind from the cuffs, the Beholder said, "How do you know I will heal him?"

"Because if you don't I will kill you myself," Saqq's mom said to the Beholder in the sternest tone I've ever heard her speak.

Saqq's mom, her resolve unwavering, locked eyes with the man, her gaze fixed and filled with steely determination. Her voice held a firmness brooking no argument, demanding compliance and trust in equal measure. She wielded her words like a weapon, a shield against any wavering resolve.

The man's lips curled into a bitter smile, a silent acknowledgment of the intricate dance of power and vulnerability playing out before him. He understood the gravity of the request, the enormity of the act he was being asked to perform. The room seemed to hold its breath, waiting for his response. Finally, with a reluctant nod, he agreed to the task. The air shifted, charged with a mix of relief and trepidation. A fragile truce had been forged, tethering the fates of the man, Saqq's father, and our own intertwined destinies.

We carefully transported Saqq's father downstairs, our movements gentle yet urgent. The makeshift gurney creaked under the weight of our hopes and a life teetering on the edge. The descent felt like a descent into the depths of the unknown, each step echoing with the uncertainty of what lay ahead.

As we reached the holding cell of the Beholder, the atmosphere shifted. The room pulsed with an otherworldly energy, as if the very walls were alive with anticipation. Saqq's mom approached the man, unlocking his restraints with a calculated mixture of trust and caution.

The Beholder, his face etched with a blend of weariness and resignation, knelt beside Saqq's father. The air grew charged, heavy with the weight of expectation. The room seemed to hold its breath, as if time itself held still to witness the unfolding act of redemption. Clapping his hands with a rhythm that carried echoes of forgotten power, the Beholder conjured a concentrated fireball of energy. Its searing heat danced in the air, casting eerie shadows on the walls. With deft movements, he placed the scorching fireball over Saqq's father's wound, guiding its healing power with a touch that was equal parts gentleness and command.

The room bathed in a warm, pulsating glow as the Beholder wove his magic. A palpable energy radiated from the very core of his being, intertwining with the wounded man's essence. The air crackled with the intensity of the moment, a delicate dance between life and death, despair and hope.

With each pass of his hand, the wound responded, its jagged edges knitting together. A sense of awe washed over us as we witnessed the miracle unfold before our eyes. The scab formed a protective barrier against further harm, a testament to the power of healing and the resilience of the human spirit.

As the Beholder rose to his feet, his gaze met Saqq's mom's unwavering stare. The room seemed to hold its breath, a collective exhale of relief and gratitude. The bonds of the past were not easily severed, but in that moment, a seed of redemption was planted.

Silently, without a word, the Beholder acknowledged his debt repaid. With a final nod, he retreated into the shadows, his presence fading like a phantom. The room, now imbued with a sense of hope and possibility, brimmed with a renewed determination to face the challenges laying ahead.

"There, he will live. Give it until the morning and he will be in good shape in no time. It's been a nice little reunion, and I've kept my end of the deal. Can I go now? I have to get to my wife and daughter," the Beholder explained.

"Before you go, I don't want to ever see you near my home, near my family, or Shaylah's family. If we see you, we will kill you. Now go," Saqq's mom commanded.

"Geneva and Geni, I'm coming," the Beholder said as he bolted out of the house.

"Did he just say Geni and Geneva? You mean, Geni Port is his daughter?" I said in disbelief.

We stood there, bathed in the glow of a newfound hope, watching Saqq's father heal before our eyes. Our journey continued to unfold. The air seemed lighter, infused with a sense of purpose and resilience. The path ahead may be treacherous, but with the beacon of healing guiding our way, we pressed on, united in our quest for justice and the triumph of light over darkness.

We helped transport Saqq's father to the SUV as a plan formed in my mind. We needed to reach Kaman Plaza without attracting attention. "Saqq, we'll need your mom to drive us to the pool," I declared, taking charge of the situation.

Saqq's parents' SUV became our vessel, and together, we set off toward Kaman Plaza, praying that stealth and speed would be our allies in this perilous journey.

Chapter 18

Shaylah

We all managed to cram into the SUV, Saqq's dad resting and healing just as the Beholder had predicted. Tray used Na'Ray's cell phone to call her parents and assure them she was safe. Saqq's mom turned off the SUV's lights as we approached the pool, and Saqq bid his parents farewell with hugs and kisses before leaving the car.

The swimming pool security guard, dozing off at his desk, remained oblivious to our stealthy movements as we crawled one by one across the floor to reach the locker rooms. Inside, Na'Ray playfully teased Dash and Saqq about finding themselves in the same space as us. Once we made it out of the locker room, I noticed the hole where I stashed my wet clothes was tampered with, and my belongings were missing. Someone had clearly seen me hide them. The mystery of the missing items gnawed at me, leaving me with unanswered questions.

"We need to swim to the deep end. Once we're there, I have to turn the four corners. This will trigger an opening, causing the water to drain. We can then slide through the drain into the other side," I informed everyone, eager to move forward.

Having twisted three of the corners, I realized one was still missing. Without hesitation, I pulled out my dagger and wedged it into the groove, turning the corner backward. As the water began to drain, we each slid through the opening, one by one. After sealing off the drain, we noticed an unusual abundance of footprints in the area, which hadn't been there when I first entered. In fact, there were only my footprints. The sheer number of prints heading in the opposite direction of our tunnel, indicated a large group had passed through.

Time was of the essence, and although we knew danger lurked nearby, their diversion in the opposite direction bought us a few precious minutes to navigate the tunnel system back to the Kaman Plaza. The distant sound of helicopters and the discussions of evacuations nearby confirmed Kaman Plaza was drawing closer.

At a storm drain, we paused to listen to passersby talking about the evacuation and expressing concern for our family. A woman even stopped to pray for us in the middle of the street, eliciting a mix of emotions in those witnessing her act of compassion. Jackson, a familiar face, was among the crowd, desperately searching for his family.

"Look, it's Jackson. He's screaming for Geni and Geneva," I said. "I sure hope he remembers how well your parents treated him when he reunites with them. Come on, we gotta keep moving. We're almost there."

With limited time we pressed toward the drain leading to Kaman Plaza. Approaching the drain pipe, I could see my footprints were the only ones visible, leaving no trace of anyone else's. Placing a lit wick by the opening, I signaled Daddy on the other side to open the drain. With relief, I climbed through, followed by Tray and Saqq and walked toward the portal where everyone else was standing waiting for us.

As Dash knelt to give Na'Ray a boost, two men suddenly attacked them from behind. Na'Ray's voice echoed through the chaos, urging me to go as the countdown began. Fueled by adrenaline and determination, I sprinted toward the drain.

"No I have to save Na'Ray and Dash," I insisted to Daddy, bolting toward the drain to help them.

Through the chaos, I witnessed Na'Ray poised to throw the Tetratetum toward me. Just as she launched it into the air, an explosion erupted, causing the roots and protective shield to come crashing down, along with the building itself.

When I regained consciousness, the world around me was a cacophony of ringing in my ears and blurred vision. I shook my head and wiped my eyes, hoping to regain clarity. The gray sky loomed overhead, smog polluting the air and obscuring my surroundings. I surveyed the scene, debris scattered across the burned patch of grass, and lifeless trees standing in the distance.

A sense of familiarity washed over me, and I realized where we were. Charcantium. Tears streamed down Momma's face, and Daddy tried to console her as I searched for Dash and Na'Ray, calling their names. Momma's tears intensified upon seeing my anguish, and she cried even harder.

"We lost Dash, Na'Ray and the Tetratetum? What do we do now?" I sobbed, the weight of grief overwhelming me. Daddy embraced me tightly, trying his best to offer comfort.

I couldn't shake the image of Na'Ray launching the Tetratetum toward me just before the explosion. Rage consumed me, and I yearned to seek revenge on the Parjeks for the lives of my brother and sister.

Amid the turmoil, Grandma Caly Rose walked over from the group surrounding Uncle Ytwen, who lay unconscious on the ground. He was the last of us to pass through the portal door. The intensity of the blast violently flung him to the ground like a ragdoll.

Everyone was surrounding Uncle Ytwen. Grandma Caly Rose frantically checked him for signs of life. Auntie Vania knelt down beside Grandma Caly Rose and placed her hand on Uncle Ytwen's chest. She closed her eyes and placed her other hand on his chest as well.

"He's still alive. I feel his spirit returning to his physical body," Auntie Vania explained.

Uncle Ytwen simultaneously opened his eyes and gasped for air. Grandma Caly Rose wasted no time hugging him as he struggled to sit up from his injuries. I was relieved he was alive and so was everyone else. Our rejoicing was cut short as Auntie Vania stood with panic all over her face.

"We must leave immediately; they are heading this way," Aunt Vania urged, her voice filled with urgency.

We gathered our belongings and followed Aunt Vania into the woods, seeking refuge and staying out of sight. From our hiding spot, we observed a line of men, women, children, and livestock herded by the Parjeks. Grandma Caly Rose's despair was evident as she turned to Aunt Vania, seeking answers.

"What is happening, Vania? Where are they taking them?" Grandma Caly Rose's voice quivered with concern.

"The Parjeks claimed our fertile lands, our communities, and our resources. They banished all Jewels to the most inhospitable parts of Charcantium. This is the trail of the remaining Jewels Beholders who fought valiantly to stay on their land," Aunt Vania explained, her words laced with sorrow.

"But there's no water or sustenance there. Nothing can grow. They won't survive for much longer," Grandma Caly Rose lamented.

"That is the Parjeks' goal. They want to exterminate all of us. It gets worse, Momma. When the moon rises, they can control the roots. They've learned how to manipulate them, turning them into instruments of evil during their most vulnerable hours. The roots snatch Jewels at random, burying them alive underground. No one is safe. There is nothing we can do to fight back. No weapons to protect ourselves from the roots or the Parjeks. They believe Daddy holds the key to the Tetratetum, but he won't tell them where it is. If they knew, I'm certain they would kill him once they obtain its contents." Grandma Caly Roses' anguish deepened as she absorbed Aunt Vania's words.

"What will they do with the Beholders?" Grandma Caly Rose inquired, her voice heavy with worry.

"The remaining Beholders turned on us and aligned themselves with the Parjeks. They chose lands for themselves and are rebuilding their communities as we speak. They started retelling our stories, distorting the truth and discrediting the Jewels' contributions to Charcantium," Aunt Vania revealed.

"We must find RaKem. Where are they holding him?" Grandma Caly Rose's determination resurfaced.

"They are heavily guarding him inside the cave at Mt. Charcantium."

Grandma Caly Rose, Momma and Daddy stayed behind with the elders to watch over our people, rescuing as many as possible in the hours leading up to nightfall. Meanwhile, Saqq and Tray were led through the woods, following Aunt Vania's lead toward Mt. Charcantium to rescue Grandpa RaKem.

For what felt like hours, we trekked through the dense forest, our senses heightened by the surroundings. The path ahead revealed itself, beckoning us to move forward. Aunt Vania, aware of the lurking danger, knew she couldn't continue the journey with us or her cover would be blown and we would all be in danger. She hugged each of us tightly before blending in with the line of marching Parjeks heading in the opposite direction.

The path we walked upon was strewn with massive, partially burned brown roots, remnants of the recent chaos. We carefully crossed streams, balancing ourselves on fallen trees, and kept a vigilant watch for any hidden Parjeks patrolling the woods. The night sky cast an eerie glow above us as we ventured deeper into the forest, our destination drawing nearer. The distant sound of helicopters echoed through the air, signifying the presence of imminent danger.

We halted our march, seeking cover near a massive tree trunk, as a family, led by armed Parjeks, came into view. One of the Parjeks, looking up at the sky, rejoiced at the arrival of nightfall. With his head raised and a few words uttered, an evil laugh escaped his lips, prompting the others to follow suit, backing away from the defenseless family.

Strong tremors rumbled beneath our feet, threatening to knock us off balance. Thick white roots burst from the ground, encircling the terrified family. The Parjeks laughed as they moved away, leaving the helpless victims to their fate. One of the roots coiled tightly around the smallest child, while the parents desperately tried to free her.

Standing by was not an option, not after what Grandpa RaKem showed me in my dream. I signaled Saqq and Tray to prepare for a confrontation with the Parjeks, assuming defensive positions while keeping a wary eye on the rogue roots. Raising my hand toward the moonlit sky, I allowed its energy to flow through me, charging my bracelet. It glowed with a luminous intensity as I slammed my hand down, causing the ground to quake even more fiercely than the Parjek's spell. The deadly root released its grip, retreating into the earth.

The family quickly gathered their children, and I instructed them to head toward the nearby river. The remaining rogue roots followed behind, slithering into openings created in the ground. The chaos caught the attention of other Parjeks nearby.

A beam of blue light struck a nearby tree, creating a gaping hole as the scent of burning wood filled the air. The Parjeks fired their weapons relentlessly in our direction, their firepower formidable. Saqq, seizing an opportunity, moved swiftly toward the left side of the forest, subduing one of the Parjeks from behind with a sizable boulder. Unconscious, the Parjek crumpled to the ground, and Saqq seized his weapons, firing back at the encroaching Parjeks with precise accuracy. Five Parjeks fell to his expertise, eliminated by the scepter they wielded. We collected the discarded weapons, arming ourselves, before heading toward the river alongside the family we rescued.

At the river's edge, the father tended to his family's wounds, caused by the roots' grip. The youngest girl cried out in pain as her mother carefully wrapped her wounds with makeshift bandages, using wet leaves to soothe the injuries.

"Thank you. You saved our lives," the father said gratefully. "Who are you? I've never seen any of you here before."

"My name is Shaylah. Shaylah Marston. My grandfather is RaKem. I need to find him. We were headed to Mt. Charcantium when we saw you and your family in the woods with the Parjeks. I have to get to Mt. Charcantium," I said to the man.

"You're RaKem's granddaughter. The Jewel from the legend who is supposed to come and save Charcantium," he said. "Well, I'm a believer. My name is Joseph. We are Jewels, too. You saved my family. I owe you my life. The path we were on was crawling with Parjeks. Many families like us refused to leave our homes, standing our ground against the invaders. But we were outnumbered, and their weapons proved superior."

Joseph continued, recounting the horrors of the rogue roots, snatching countless men, women, and children, and the desperate fight they put up until overwhelmed by the Parjeks. The trauma in his voice was palpable, proof of his resilience and determination not to let the Parjeks or the roots claim him or his loved ones without a fight.

"To get to Mt. Charcantium, follow this river. I must warn you, the area is heavily patrolled by Parjeks. But you will have a vantage point to spot them before they spot you, giving you a chance to take cover until it's safe or to take them out," Joseph shared, accepting the scepters I handed him and his wife.

Grateful for Joseph's guidance, I thanked him before he gathered his family and disappeared into the opposite direction. We, on the other hand, continued along the river, navigating the treacherous path with caution. The moon above cast an ethereal glow, illuminating our way and heightening our senses, as we marched closer to Mt. Charcantium and the challenges awaiting us.

Chapter 19

Shaylah

W alking alongside the babbling stream, pebbles beneath my feet, my mind was consumed by thoughts of Na'Ray and Dash. The pain of their loss weighed heavily on my heart, threatening to spill forth as tears welled in my eyes. I kept my head down, wiping away the evidence of my grief before Tray and Saqq could notice. As we neared the widening of the stream, tall trees parted, revealing the majestic presence of Mt. Charcantium. Its grandeur loomed before us, casting a mesmerizing spell upon our senses, momentarily halting us in silent awe.

"We have arrived, this is Mt. Charcantium," I whispered to Tray and Saqq, concealing my sorrow for the moment.

Tray's observant eyes captured the true scale of the mountain. "Shay, this mountain is huge. Way bigger than anything I have ever seen or imagined. How do we even begin to climb to the summit?"

Tray was right, the journey to the peak seemed insurmountable, and time was not on our side. The weight of our mission, to reach my Grandpa RaKem, weighed heavily on me, as Momma, Daddy and Grandma Caly Rose depended on us. Firmly gripping our weapons, we pressed forward, determined to find a way up the mountain. However, Saqq's keen hearing caught a faint sound, causing us to pause.

A horse-drawn wagon appeared on the path, its wheels creaking, a lone occupant shackled and in desperate shape forcefully being pulled behind. The man's tattered clothes bore the stains of blood and dirt, and the clinking of rusty chains emphasized his captivity. Saqq swiftly reacted, firing his scepter at the chains, causing them to break and the man to stumble to the side of the path. The wagon came to a halt, and two Parjeks jumped out, armed and ready. They rushed toward the shackled man, inspecting the damaged chains.

"What happened? How did the chains break like this?" demanded the Parjek, his fist landing brutally on the defenseless man's face.

"I swear, I didn't do it. I had no part in it. I don't know how they broke," pleaded the helpless man, his voice laced with fear.

Saqq and I retaliated, firing our scepters at the Parjeks. My shot found its mark, toppling one of the Parjeks to the ground. Saqq's target evaded the scorching beam and fired back in our direction. The searing heat struck Saqq's shoulder, and he crumpled to the ground in pain. The Parjek, using the helpless man as a shield, warned us to drop our weapons and step out into the open, threatening to kill the man if we refused. Helplessly, Saqq and I complied, walking toward the open space, dropping our weapons along the way. The Parjek pushed the man to the ground, pointing his scepter menacingly in our direction, demanding answers.

"Who are you? What brings you here?" he barked, his eyes burning with suspicion.

Before he could utter another word, Tray emerged from behind him, firing her weapon and causing him to collapse to the ground. He was injured and unconscious, but not dead. We rushed to the aid of the shackled man, removing the chains binding him and placing them on the fallen Parjek. Gently, we helped the injured man to his feet, and together we loaded the Parjek's unconscious body into the back of the wagon.

"Thank you young folks for freeing me from the Parjeks. I was attempting to reach the mountain to rescue my brother. I had a vision of a hidden passageway but Parjeks patrolling these trails captured me."

"Your brother?" I asked, intrigued.

"Yes, my brother, RaKem. They've held him captive at the summit of this mountain for over fourteen years. Enough is enough. RaKem begged me not to attempt a rescue, no matter the circumstances. But our people are dying, the roots have turned against us and the Parjeks have seized our lands. We cannot reclaim what is rightfully ours without him. We cannot wait for the prophecy to be fulfilled. We need my brother now," the injured man confided, his voice filled with desperation.

A pang of guilt and remorse washed over me. I longed to reveal my true identity, but the words remained trapped in my throat. Saqq and Tray respected my silence, not pressuring me to disclose the weighty secret I carried.

"I'm sorry, my name is Emmerson. You can call me Unk."

"Nice to meet you, Unk. I'm Shay, this is Tray and Saqq. Now we must get going so we can help you find your brother."

I assured Unk we would assist him in finding the hidden passageway inside the mountain to reunite him with his brother, my Grandpa RaKem.

I hurried to the back of the wagon with Tray, the urgency of our mission propelling us forward. Unk, his expression a mix of confusion and curiosity, watched us intently, but we didn't pause to ask any more questions as time was not on our side. Together, Tray and I secured the injured Parjek in the back of the wagon, ensuring his safety as best we could. Meanwhile, Saqq and Unk took the reins and guided the wagon, their focus unwavering.

The journey up the mountain was tumultuous, the wagon shaking and jerking as we navigated the rugged terrain. With each bump and jolt, our determination grew stronger, fueling our resolve to reach our destination. Finally, we reached a stopping point, and Saqq and Unk hurried to assist Tray and me out of the wagon. As a team, we released the horse and carefully concealed the wagon within a massive bush, ensuring it would remain hidden from prying eyes. We bound the injured unconscious Parjek to the tree nearby and continued on our trek.

Guided by Unk, we approached a massive crack in the side of the mountain. His eyes scanned the area, ever vigilant for any sign of danger. With practiced hands, he retrieved a weathered leather rope and a rusty copper hinged bolt from within the crack. With precision, he secured the bolt, causing the crack to widen, sending a cloud of dust and debris into the air. The opening beckoned us, jagged and foreboding, yet wide enough for us to pass through, one by one.

Stepping into the belly of the mountain, we found ourselves engulfed in darkness. The cool, damp air clung to our skin and the ground beneath our feet felt slightly slick. To combat the darkness, Saqq and Tray activated their scepters, casting a fiery blue glow illuminating our surroundings. The walls of the cave, adorned with sparkling dark green moss, seemed to come alive in the flickering light.

Unk's voice called us over, drawing our attention to a wall scone embedded within the rock. Time had weathered it, leaving it rusted and seemingly nonfunctional. Unk ran his finger across its surface, inspecting it closely. Then, with Saqq standing at a safe distance, Unk unleashed the power of the scepter upon the scone. A spark ignited, traveling from scone to scone in a mesmerizing cascade of light. The path before us illuminated, leading us further up the mountain.

Narrow rock slabs jutted out from the sides of the wall, forming a treacherous staircase. Saqq tested the first step, his determination unyielding. Unk, our anchor, provided support, while Tray and I took our place in the middle, ensuring we were there for one another. In silence, we ascended, our steps careful and deliberate, each movement carrying the weight of our purpose.

Midway up the mountain, our progress came to a halt as Saqq's keen eyes caught sight of hieroglyphics adorning the rock face. Unk's voice resonated softly, recounting the legend of Charcantium's creation. Step by step, he shared the stories of the Darkest Lights, their names rolling off his tongue with reverence. One depiction caught my eye, a beautiful figure with striking similarities to myself. Enthralled, I lost my footing, the scepter slipping from my grasp, and I teetered perilously close to the edge.

Fear gripped me, but in that moment, Unk's swift action saved me from a tragic fate. Scaling the wall with agility, he extended his hand, gripping mine tightly and pulling me to safety.

"We can't afford to lose any of you. You all saved my life. Glad to save yours, Shaylah. Now, pay attention and keep moving. We're almost at the top."

"Thank you, Unk. That was close." Gratitude washed over me.

With renewed determination, we continued our ascent, reaching the summit of the mountain. As we stood upon the platform, my gaze fell upon a familiar face depicted on the wall. It was Grandpa RaKem, a younger and more regal version than the one I had seen in my dreams. Unk's voice carried a mixture of awe and solemnity as he acknowledged his presence, his fist raised to his chest in a gesture of solidarity.

"Brother, we are here," Unk affirmed.

Relief washed over me, knowing that the treacherous climb reached its culmination.

There was no obvious exit, but right beside Grandpa RaKem's drawing there was a cluster of reddish-brown roots covering the small section of the wall. I walked over to the area to get a closer look. Through the roots, I noticed there was another drawing of some sort.

"What's that, Shay?" Tray inquired, as she walked toward my direction.

"There's something behind all of these roots. Use the scepter."

Expecting the scorching heat to melt away the roots, we were taken aback when they remained unscathed. Apprehensively, I reached out to touch the roots. The gemstone on my bracelet glimmered the closer my hand got, glowing uninterrupted as my hand glided over the roots. They simultaneously unwound from around each other. The cracking and popping noise startled us all. I was in awe, touching the roots as they unfroze becoming fully animated. They whisked me around, suspending me over the edge of the ledge. Unk uneasily yelled and attempted to pull me back down to safety. It was at that moment I realized I was not afraid and was enjoying the connection I felt with the roots. The roots softly brought me back down to the ledge facing the wall. The drawing hidden behind them was revealed.

"Shay, that looks a lot like you," Saqq pointed out.

He was right. It was a spitting image of me, right down to the bracelet on my wrist. But the drawing on the bracelet had three grooves instead of one as I only had one of the three Charcantium crystals. Saqq and I continued to look at the depiction of me on the wall as Unk slowly approached.

"This can't be? Why you? You're the one my brother told me about all those years ago. The Darkest Light who can control the rogue roots," Unk recounted. But his rejoicing turned to a more somber tone. "I begged RaKem to use his powers that night. He wouldn't. Not for me. Not for anyone. He promised Charcantium would survive this onslaught of all-out carnage by the Parjeks when the most powerful Darkest Light this realm has birthed, comes forward to take their rightful place. I promised to never enter until I received a sign. I waited year after year for a sign. Almost giving up hope because I had no clue what sign to look for. That was until I had a vision yesterday of the secret passageway and to head to the mountain knowing that I could be killed by the Parjeks. I did it anyway and was captured, tortured, and beaten inches from death. That's when you and your friends came along and saved my life. I was suspicious of you and your friends but, deep down inside, I wanted you to help me save my brother."

"Unk, I'm sorry I didn't tell you who I was. We've been fighting since we got here. When I saw you chained, I knew we had to help. My name is Shaylah Marston. I am the granddaughter of RaKem and Caly Rose Marston. Daughter of Michael and Moonia Marston. I am Darkest Light," I said pointing to the drawing on the wall.

Unk whisked me into his arms, lifting me off the ground. He thanked our ancestors that birthed beyond this universe for allowing him to be a part of this historic moment. I was impressed by the strength he had at his age to pick me up after being nearly beaten to death by the Parjeks.

With a sense of purpose burning within me, I knew my destiny awaited. The mountain unveiled its secrets, and now it was time to embrace my role as the Darkest Light.

However, Tray interjected, reminding us of the urgency of our mission.

"I hate to interrupt this touching family reunion, but we must keep moving."

We stood on a ledge within the mountain before the wall bearing my likeness. Twisted roots intertwined, forming a pointed extension aligning with one of the grooves on the wall. Tentatively, I ran my hand along the groove, and the Charcantium crystal on my wrist fractured, embedding itself within the groove. The crystal shifted, aligning with the final groove, causing the wall bearing my image to crack and crumble. As the dust settled, the animated roots beckoned us forward, leading the way deeper into the mountain.

Chapter 20

Shaylah

The roots, like obedient guardians, guided us deeper into the cavernous interior of the rocky mountain top. The air grew cool and damp, wrapping around us like a whispering shroud. As we ventured forth, the scene unfolding before us deviated from Grandma Caly Rose's vivid descriptions. Instead of glistening emeralds adorning the walls, shards of broken fragments lay scattered, their brilliance dimmed by time and neglect. And the once-beautiful blue waters she spoke of had long since evaporated, leaving behind a desolate emptiness.

"What happened here? Where's the water?"

Questions tumbled from my lips, their urgency echoing through the cavern, only to fall silent as my gaze fixed upon a figure crumpled in the far corner. Bound and restrained, a man lay motionless, his identity shrouded beneath a black covering. Unk's desperation was palpable as he rushed to the man's side, unveiling his face with trembling hands. Emmerson's voice, filled with hope and anguish, called out to his brother. But the response was a deafening silence, broken only by the sound of Unk's persistent shaking.

"Ra. Ra. It's me, Emmerson. Ra. Wake up brother. We're here," Unk assured.

Together, we worked diligently to free RaKem from the heavy, rusted chains binding him as he hardly moved to acknowledge our presence. With each clink and rattle, our determination grew stronger, the weight of anticipation heavy in the air. Finally, as the last restraint fell away, RaKem stirred, his consciousness gradually returning. Dry coughs racked his weakened frame as Unk gently propped him against the cool cave wall, offering a modicum of support.

In the enveloping darkness, Saqq and Tray summoned the power of their scepters, creating a gentle luminescence casting ethereal light upon our surroundings. Within this dim glow, we could now see RaKem's battered visage, his injuries attesting to the trials he endured. His face bore the marks of dried blood mingled with dirt, a stark contrast against his pale complexion. One eye remained swollen shut, while a deep gash marred the side of his swollen cheek.

With a tenderness born of brotherhood, Unk tore a strip of cloth from his own shirt, gently dabbing at the blood seeping from the cut above RaKem's eyebrow. The feeble light revealed the pained squint in RaKem's eyes as he struggled to adjust to the brightness emanating from the scepters. Unk's concerned words washed over him, unanswered, as RaKem's gaze fixed upon me, his voice barely a whisper.

"Shaylah." The word escaped his lips, carrying with it a mixture of shock and recognition. In that moment, speech eluded me, swallowed by a whirlwind of emotions. But I summoned the strength to nod, affirming my identity. A fleeting smile etched itself upon RaKem's worn features, illustrating his enduring love and pride.

A soft, pained moan escaped Grandpa RaKem's lips, resonating with a depth of emotion compelling me to kneel by his side. His trembling hand reached out, brushing against my cheek in a tender gesture. "Still the same bright-eyed girl I met all those years ago," he murmured. "I've been waiting for you. I sensed the energy every time you used the Charcantium crystal I left behind. It reverberated through us all, even the Parjeks. Shaylah, you possess a power beyond measure. You are the chosen one, the most formidable Darkest Light to ever grace our realm."

Emmerson, captivated by his brother's rekindled memories, expressed his gratitude for our timely arrival. His words held the weight of a pivotal moment, a realization that our presence had shifted the course of fate. "Michael and I devised the Tetratetum as a diversion, a veiled enchantment to mislead those unworthy of the rogue roots' power. The true magic resided within the Book of Jewels, the most powerful tool in our lineage's arsenal. It is sealed with the blood of every Jewel and every Darkest Light that ever existed. The Book of Jewels will amplify your power one million times over. I entrusted the book to Caly Rose and I'm so thankful she kept it safe all these years. The passage you recited, 'earth bend and water flow, I conjure roots as I go. Light as the air and heavy as the sea, bestow your powers unto me,' serves as a key to unlock the depths of your potential. Only a Jewel worthy of the Darkest Light's powers could harness that kind of birthright power to command the rogue roots."

Grandpa RaKem's voice carried a profound weight of regret as he continued, recounting the sacrifices and losses endured in the long wait for this day. "Waiting came at a heavy cost, the lives of countless Jewels. I had to give the Parjeks something to appease their hunger for power. I revealed to them the weakness of the rogue roots—moonlight. Under its shimmering glow, the roots could be manipulated for dark intentions. And that's precisely what they did. They commanded the roots to drag Jewels underground indiscriminately. If I had disclosed the whereabouts of Caly Rose, the Book of Jewels, and the Tetratetum, they would have snuffed out your life before you could claim your rightful place as the Darkest Light."

A sense of remorse tinged Grandpa RaKem's words, an acknowledgment of the sacrifices made to protect the legacy of the Darkest Light.

Meanwhile, the rogue roots, attuned to the disturbance at the entrance of the cave, sprang into action. Like a living entity, they surged forward, weaving together to form a formidable barrier, enveloping the cave in an impenetrable darkness. The Parjeks' shouts echoed through the obsidian veil as they clashed with the defiant roots, their weapons clashing futilely against the resilient guardians.

"Where is Caly Rose?" He looked at Unk and I for answers.

Just as he asked, an explosion rocked the cave damaging the roots at the entryway of the cave. As the powerful explosion reverberated through the cave,

Tray and Saqq grabbed their scepters, blazing them with intense fiery light. Unk and I rushed to support Grandpa RaKem, aiding him as he struggled to his feet. Yet, before we could react, another deafening blast shook the cavern, sending tremors through the very foundation of the rock.

Chunks of large, shattered stone cascaded down, chaos descending upon us. We sought shelter, but it was futile as the cave crumbled around us. I found myself trapped beneath a colossal boulder, its weight pressing down mercilessly. Agony lanced through my body as my pelvis crumpled under the immense pressure, and both my legs were shattered, immobilizing me completely. A strangled cry escaped my lips as I called out for help, my voice trembling with fear.

In that moment, as darkness threatened to consume me, a glimmer of hope emerged. Tray, battered and injured, reached out her trembling hand toward mine, wordlessly conveying her unwavering solidarity. A massive boulder pinned her down beside me, her face marred by deep scrapes and her left eye swollen shut. Though blood spilled from her mouth, she attempted to utter words of reassurance. Tears streamed down my cheeks, mingling with the dust and debris, as the weight of our predicament settled upon me.

In that desperate, heartbreaking moment, the specter of mortality loomed over us, threatening to extinguish our spirits.

I don't want to die like this.

"'Tray stay with me. Traylecia stay with me please," I begged as I desperately tried to free myself from the boulder crushing me to help her. Tray cried louder as she heard the despair in my voice. Lying on my back, I felt a cool puddle forming beneath me. I looked over at Tray again. Her body glowed as it was partially covered in the water. She turned her head away from me, resting her head back into the water.

"No Tray don't." I watched helplessly as she fully submerged her head back into the water.

Is this it? The legacy of the Marstons. Death by drowning.

In that heart-wrenching moment, I turned my gaze to Tray, seeking solace in her presence, but she had slipped away from this realm. The weight of her absence settled upon me like a heavy cloak, the void left by her departure unfathomable.

As the waters of the cave rose around me, a curious warmth enveloped my weary body, offering a strange comfort. With each passing second, I gave in to the embrace of the liquid, surrendering to the inevitable. In the depths of my despair, I no longer fought against my fate, allowing myself to sink deeper into the soothing depths.

Suddenly, the cave quivered once again, a symphony of movement re-verberating through the air. Boulders, once immovable giants, were lifted effortlessly as if they were mere feathers dancing upon the wind. The water surged in a frenzied whirlpool, spinning and twirling with a raw, untamed energy. And there, amid the tumult, the rogue roots burst forth from the ground, their tendrils reaching out as if in a desperate attempt to rescue us from our unconscious state.

Grandpa RaKem, Unk, Tray, Saqq, and I, all lying motionless, were caught in the swirling maelstrom. The water cradled our fragile forms, carrying us along its current, while the roots, with a determined purpose, coiled around each of us individually. With a gentle strength, they pulled us down, deep into the earth, our bodies disappearing beneath the surface.

The cave faded from view as the water continued its relentless dance, spinning us around like fragments of debris caught in the eye of a storm. Yet, in this extraordinary moment, a miraculous transformation took place. The water, with its ethereal touch, worked its mystical wonders, mending every wound and setting right every broken bone. Its healing essence flowed through our beings, bestowing upon us a renewed vitality.

And so, as the cave trembled and the roots guided our descent, a veil of darkness enveloped us, obscuring the world above. We embarked on an unseen journey, a passage into the unknown, where the forces of nature and magic intertwined, leading us to a realm beyond comprehension.

Where are we?

We descended into a tranquil pool of crystal-clear water, its sparkling blue hues mirroring the tales woven by Grandma Caly Rose. Yet, the surroundings were far from familiar, casting an otherworldly air upon the scene.

Tray emerged from the water, her voice laden with curiosity. "What just happened?" she queried, stepping closer to me. I embraced her tightly, a wave of relief washing over me as I saw Saqq, Unk, and Grandpa RaKem standing alongside us. They, too, appeared transformed, their regal presence radiating an aura of restoration belying the injuries they endured.

As we took in our surroundings, figures materialized from the depths of the darkness, their forms emerging with a purposeful grace. Grandpa RaKem motioned for us to remain calm, assuring us these were the individuals pulled underground by the very roots the Parjeks deemed a death sentence. What the Parjeks did not comprehend was the roots' inherent limitation—they were forbidden from killing Jewels, their purpose solely to safeguard them below the surface. Unk's jubilation swelled upon this revelation, his heart rejoicing at the reunion with his beloved wife, Vella, one of the first Jewels to be embraced by the roots' protective grasp.

With a resolute determination, Grandpa RaKem ascended a stone slab, commanding the attention of all those gathered. His voice carried through the stillness, resonating with the weight of his words. "Jewels of Charcantium, there were secrets I could not share, even as I surrendered to the Parjeks and unveiled the roots' manipulation under the moonlight, without the aid of Charcantium crystals. They remained unaware of my decree—no Jewel shall perish by the roots' hand, but rather be drawn beneath the earth to ensure their safety until the true Darkest Light revealed herself. And now, behold, my granddaughter Shaylah Marston, the embodiment of the Darkest Light herself."

A hush settled over the assembly, their gaze fixed upon me, their faces awash with awe and reverence. In that poignant moment, silence reigned supreme, each breath heavy with anticipation.

"You mean to tell me we've been stuck down here in partial darkness, waiting for your estranged teenage granddaughter?" Mesha, the widow of a fallen Jewel soldier, voiced her frustrations. "I've lost count of the years we've spent down here. Some have endured fourteen long years, while others have only known this darkness for days. Our survival has depended on moss, bugs, and rodents we could scrounge for sustenance. Every time someone gets pulled down, we hope the roots bring food with them."

Grandpa RaKem stood his ground, defending his decisions against the torrent of questions and doubts thrown his way. The intensity of the conversation escalated and my restlessness grew.

"It hasn't been easy for any of us. But we are alive because of my granddaughter," Grandpa RaKem interjected, his voice filled with a mix of determination and weariness. "And so are you," he said, pointing in Mesha's direction.

"She is the one!" Aunt BJ's voice rang out, breaking the tension. Her presence brought a sense of familiarity and trust amid the Jewels' suspicions about Grandpa RaKem's revelation of my true identity.

"Aunt BJ, why are you down here?" I inquired, genuinely concerned for her well-being as she stood before me, nursing her injuries.

"We launched an attack on the Parjeks along the trail, freeing as many Jewels as we could," Aunt BJ explained. "The roots surrounded Caly Rose, and in a split-second decision, I pushed her out of harm's way, sacrificing myself unknowingly. Little did I know, the roots would carry me below and grant me life."

"What about the others?" I pressed, eager to ensure the safety of Momma, Daddy, and Grandma Caly Rose.

"I'm unsure of their fate, but we need to go back to the trail leading to the uninhabitable land where the Parjeks hold the rest of your people captive. That's where we will find Caly Rose," Aunt BJ replied, her gaze unwavering.

I signaled to the roots, commanding them to create an opening in the ground. As the earth shifted and settled, a glimpse of the morning sky emerged. Saqq and Tray, understanding my impatience, stepped through the opening, their scepters ablaze with power. Grandpa RaKem and the able-bodied men followed suit, while the women and children emerged last, prodded by the roots' gentle guidance.

Saqq and Tray remained behind, tending to the women and children near the stream by the mountain, while the rest of us embarked on our journey to the uninhabitable land where our captive kin awaited rescue.

Chapter 21

Shaylah

Not too far into our treacherous trek, we arrived at the Trail of Jewels. My heart swelled with relief as I laid eyes on Daddy, Momma, and Grandma Caly. Their bodies were weary and battered, their faces etched with exhaustion and determination. They were chained together, bound by the cruel constraints imposed by the Parjeks. Despite their injuries, they pushed forward, a testament to their unwavering strength.

Grandpa RaKem, his eyes filled with a mixture of pride and concern, wasted no time. With a simple nod in my direction, he signaled it was time to act. The rogue roots, sensing our collective resolve, burst forth from the ground with a thunderous force. They coiled and twisted, their reddish-brown tendrils snaking through the air, reaching for the Parjeks with a ferocity fueled by our shared desire for liberation.

Chaos erupted as the unsuspecting Parjeks found themselves ensnared in a web of roots, their movements hindered, their weapons useless against the earth's defense. They frantically tried to retrieve their scepters, their faces contorted with a mix of rage and fear. But their efforts were in vain as the Jewels emerged from the shadows of the woods, launching a counterattack with a newfound determination.

Grandpa RaKem raced toward Grandma Caly Rose, his steps swift and purposeful. He endured years of separation and despair, and now he was driven by an overwhelming need to free her from her torment. I followed his lead, rushing to Daddy's side, my fingers trembling as I fumbled with the shackles binding him. The air crackled with tension as we worked with frantic urgency, each second feeling like an eternity.

"Watch out!" Momma yelled out to me. Daddy barely had time to remove the last shackle from her ankle. He was in full attack mode fighting the Parjek who just tried to kill me. Momma, with a fire in her eyes and a fierce determination, fought alongside us, her movements a blur of grace and strength. Together, we formed a united front against the onslaught of Parjeks, their numbers seemingly endless. But we would not be deterred. We fought with every ounce of our being, fueled by a love transcending time; by a determination to protect our family and our world.

I glanced at Momma, a knowing look passing between us. "I have an idea. Give me some time!" I shouted to Momma, our battle with the Parjeks still raging around us. She nodded, understanding my plan, and engaged in fierce combat, swiftly incapacitating her opponent with a high kick sending him crashing into a nearby boulder. It was my signal to proceed.

Taking a deep breath, I turned toward the towering trees, closing my eyes and summoning my inner strength. With unwavering conviction, I spoke the ancient incantation, my words resonating with power.

"Earth bend and water flow, I conjure roots as I go. Light as the air and heavy as the sea, bestow your powers unto me."

As the final words left my lips, I felt a surge of energy coursing through my body, a connection to the very essence of the elements.

In a burst of determination, I thrust my fist into the ground so forcefully it left the imprint of my hand. The earth quivered beneath me, cracking open with deep, wide fissures. Dark, thunderous clouds materialized above, crackling with whitish-blue lightning striking the ground with furious intensity. Waves of electric energy surged through each crevice, enveloping the broken roots. Massive reddish-brown roots, charged with electrifying power, emerged from the ground, intertwining and merging together with remarkable speed.

With a swift gesture, I commanded the roots to construct a formidable barricade, shielding the Jewels from the relentless onslaught of the Parjeks' weapons. Grandpa RaKem and Daddy swiftly guided the Jewels to safety, while the roots absorbed the lethal blasts, crackling with raw energy. Witnessing the Jewels finding refuge amid the protective cover of the roots, I drove my fist into the ground once more, causing the roots to grow in size, their strength and presence doubling before our eyes.

Amid the chaos, I caught a glimpse of Dash and Na'Ray, their spirits guiding us, their presence palpable. They had become ethereal guardians, watching over us from a realm beyond. Their memory infused us with a renewed sense of purpose and resilience.

From the depths of the cracks, the rogue roots pulsated with newfound vitality. They glowed with an otherworldly radiance, their reddish-brown hue infused with crackling energy. The damaged and fractured roots of Charcantium reconnected and intertwined, becoming an unyielding fortress.

I could see the weariness etched on the faces of our people, the desperate hope in their eyes. The Parjeks, once confident in their conquest, now faced a well-trained force they could not wrap their minds around. One by one, they dropped their weapons, their bravado replaced with a glimmer of understanding. They realized they were outnumbered, outmatched by the strength and unity of Charcantium.

"Leave. Return to your lands where you thrive," I commanded, my voice carrying the weight of authority and the promise of consequences. "If you ever dare to venture forth again, know that destruction, disease, disruption, and death will follow in your wake. This is your final warning," I declared, my voice resonating through the air.

The Parjeks realized the futility of their resistance. Reluctantly, their faces etched with defeat, they gathered the fallen, their comrades lost in the wake of their arrogance, and left, their departure signaling a newfound peace, a world reborn exclusive for the Jewels and Beholders of Charcantium.

As the last of the Parjeks' ships vanished into the skies on the distant horizon, the world seemed to exhale, the tension dissolving like mist. A collective sigh of relief swept through the land of Charcantium. The people, united by their resilience and unwavering spirit, rejoiced. Festivals and celebrations abounded, their jubilant atmosphere infectious.

In the days that followed, the land resounded with joyous laughter and heartfelt melodies. Feasts were held, tables groaning under the weight of sumptuous delicacies. Speeches rang out, honoring the fallen and celebrating the triumph of unity and love. Each ceremony served as a poignant tribute, a balm for our wounded hearts, a reminder of the resilience that resides within us all.

As the days turned into weeks, the people of Charcantium forged ahead, rebuilding their lives and their world. They worked tirelessly, their hands interwoven in the labor of restoration. The scars of the conflict slowly faded, replaced by signs of growth and renewal. Fields once ravaged by the Parjeks' presence blossomed with vibrant crops, their colors an ode to the resilience of the land.

Within the community, a sense of unity and camaraderie flourished. Neighbors became friends, strangers became allies, as bonds forged in the fires of adversity grew stronger. The children of Charcantium played amid laughter and joy.

For me, this newfound peace was a double-edged sword. The weight of responsibility rested heavily on my shoulders, for the power I possessed carried with it both triumph and turmoil. The legacy of the Darkest Light, passed down through generations, now coursed through my veins. I embraced my destiny, but with it came a profound sense of duty, a never-ending commitment to protect and guide my people.

In the quiet moments of reflection, I would often find solace in the memories of Dash and Na'Ray, their presence a guiding light in the depths of my soul. Their sacrifice, their unwavering love, resonated within me, fueling my determination to honor their memory and the legacy they left behind.

But even amid the pursuit of knowledge and the weight of my responsibilities, the ache persisted. They were my family, the missing pieces of my heart forever intertwined with my journey.

A bittersweet ache lingered, a longing for what could have been. I found myself stealing glances toward the woods, my heart filled with a mixture of hope and melancholy. There, amid the shadows and whispers of the trees, I searched for a sign, a flicker of Dash and Na'Ray's presence.

Time passed, and the woods held their secrets close, their depths concealing mysteries yet to be unveiled. But as I stood on the precipice of the world we fought so hard to protect, I knew the legacy of Dash and Na'Ray would forever be intertwined with our own. Their spirits would guide us, their memory etched in our hearts.

One evening, as the sun cast its golden glow upon the horizon, I stood on the edge of the woods, gazing into the depths of the unknown. The air was heavy with anticipation, as if the very fabric of Charcantium held its breath, awaiting the next chapter in our story.

In the distance, a figure emerged from the shadows, the form familiar yet ethereal. It was Dash, his eyes twinkling with mischief and warmth. Beside him stood Na'Ray, her spirit shining with a radiant energy defying explanation.

Tears welled in my eyes as they approached, their presence a balm to the ache within my soul. Dash's laughter echoed through the woods, a sound filled with the purest joy. Na'Ray's smile lit up the darkness, her grace a reminder of the strength that lay within us all.

"We are with you, Shaylah Marston," Dash's voice resonated, carrying with it the echoes of a thousand whispers. "The journey is far from over. The trials we faced were but the beginning of a grander adventure."

Na'Ray's voice, gentle and melodic, joined him. "The roots of Charcantium run deep within you, Shay. It is your destiny to guide this world toward its true potential, to bring harmony where there is discord and light where there is darkness."

As their words sank deep into my heart, I felt a surge of renewed purpose. The legacy of Charcantium, the legacy of Dash and Na'Ray, would live on through me. Together, we would navigate the uncharted paths that lay ahead, facing the challenges that awaited us with unwavering resolve.

And so, as the sun set on the horizon, casting a tapestry of colors across the sky, I took a step forward, my hands reaching out to grasp theirs. We stood united, a trinity bound by fate and love, ready to embrace the next chapter of our extraordinary journey.

The end of one adventure marked the beginning of another, and as the stars twinkled in the velvet sky, we embarked on a new quest. The path may be treacherous, the dangers ever-present, but we would face them with unwavering courage and an unbreakable bond.

For in the world of Charcantium, where magic thrives and destiny weaves its intricate tapestry, our legacy would endure. And together, guided by the spirits of those we cherished, we would shape our own destiny, forever entwined in the wonder and magic defining our extraordinary world.

Chapter 22

The End